UNDERCOVER PROTECTION

MAGGIE K. BLACK

LOVE INSPIRED SUSPENSE
INSPIRATIONAL ROMANCE

LOVE INSPIRED® SUSPENSE
INSPIRATIONAL ROMANCE

ISBN-13: 978-1-335-72258-4

Undercover Protection

Copyright © 2021 by Mags Storey

Recycling programs
for this product may
not exist in your area.

This edition published by arrangement with Harlequin Books S.A.

For questions and comments about the quality of this book, please contact us
at CustomerService@Harlequin.com.

Love Inspired
22 Adelaide St. West, 40th Floor
Toronto, Ontario M5H 4E3, Canada
www.Harlequin.com

Printed in U.S.A.

From the end of the earth will I cry unto thee, when my heart is overwhelmed: lead me to the rock that is higher than I.

—*Psalms* 61:2

A few weeks ago,
one of the most important people in my life passed away.

He'd want me to tell you that all people
are both flawed and made in the image of God,
and that we live by grace, through faith,
in community with one another.

Take a load off, Annie.

ONE

As Leia Dukes stepped through the old familiar front door of her family's darkened farmhouse, she felt a pair of beefy hands grab her roughly from behind. A second figure pulled some sort of fabric over her head to blindfold her before she could even scream. Her purse was yanked from her shoulder, and as she felt herself propelled across the floor of her childhood home, she suspected that whatever was happening to her now, farmhand Jay Brock was somehow behind it. That man had lied to her last summer, broken her heart and whatever trouble he was mixed up in might have also put her life in danger.

Save me, Lord! Nobody even knows I'm here!

Prayers for help battled the fear inside her. Why had she just shown up alone like this? Why hadn't she prepared herself for trouble?

She'd already suspected that Jay seemed like the kind of untrustworthy man who'd have enemies. Not that she'd realized that until after she'd been taken in by his good-guy routine a year ago and foolishly fallen for him. He was the reason she'd driven up from Toronto late at night to talk some sense into her sister Sally. The ruggedly handsome yet infuriatingly evasive man had been originally hired by her widower father for a few weeks last year to fix up some stuff around the century-old farm.

Secretly, she and Jay had also become such close friends that he'd actually convinced Leia he'd fallen in love with her—during a sweet whirlwind summer romance that they'd barely managed to hide from her family—before suddenly calling it off, breaking her heart, changing his phone number and disappearing from her life. Although she'd caught a glimpse of a figure who looked an awful lot like him lurking around her father's graveside last month.

Even then, she hadn't realized she might've been taken in by a con man until a colleague at the public defender's office Leia was working at to save for law school encouraged her to do some digging just in case he was wanted by the police. That's when she found out there wasn't a trace of him on social media and none of his former employers claimed to have heard of him.

Then this morning her sister Sally—who'd been driving to the now vacant farm with her new baby every few days to keep it up the best she could—had called to say that Jay had suddenly offered to get the farm ready to sell in exchange for letting him stay there. Her other sisters, who were all scattered elsewhere around the country, jumped at the proposal.

But Leia—who was both the eldest sister and the odd one out, as usual—had furiously driven up from Toronto to immediately kick him off the property, only to end up blindfolded and kidnapped.

If she ever saw Jay again, he had a whole lot to answer for.

Lord, please help me settle my heart and mind. I can't let myself get distracted thinking about him now. I need everything inside me focused on getting out of here alive.

"Where is everybody?" The voice was male, loud and so close to Leia's face she flinched.

"There's nobody here but me," she said.

As far as she knew. Her other two sisters, Rose and Quinn, lived on opposite ends of the country where they were busy scraping pennies together to throw everything into chasing their own dreams. Since it was almost midnight now, Leia didn't expect Sally would arrive until six or seven in the morning. As for one of them being the intended target, with Leia's jet-black hair and violet eyes it was utterly impossible anyone would mistake her for one of her three blonde younger sisters.

There was the cat, too, but Moses didn't live there so much as visited when he felt like it.

"Look, if this is about Jay Brock," she added, "we haven't spoken in almost a year. And I don't know anything about any kind of trouble he's in."

Nobody answered. The texture changed under her feet. She was being walked across the carpet by the man with big hands, and the faint smell of ashes told her she was nearing the fireplace. Her father had made sure that, even back when they were little girls, they knew each room, hidden door and back passage of the sprawling and isolated farmhouse like the backs of their hands. They'd all been homeschooled until high school, and he'd drilled them with games and scavenger hunts until she knew the creak of every board like the veins pumping blood to her heart.

Her dad had even taught them how to run through the house blindfolded.

And as much as she resented it when she was young—considering her father quirky, bordering on paranoid—she prayed God would help her remember what he'd taught her.

She closed her eyes, calmed her breath and tried to force herself to focus.

By the sounds of footsteps and objects crashing, she guessed there were three intruders in total. The one with the loudest boots was now tossing the place, as if searching for something, while another with big hands steered her by the shoulders. The fact they'd taken her bag meant they now had her car keys, wallet and cell phone. Were they armed? If so, then with what? Her mind reeled with unanswered questions until they threatened to drown her ability to think.

"What do you want?" Leia forced out the words over her trembling lips. "If you're here to rob us, just take what you want and go. I'm telling you we don't have much."

Just debts and a home in desperate need of repairs. If this wasn't about Jay, then why were they here? If they were thieves, why target a remote farm thirty minutes from the closest town? Yes, the property was large, but they'd never had much. Their dad had never let them buy anything new he could teach them to make or get secondhand. Even now, all four of them were up to their ears in debt and struggling to scrape up enough money to finance their dreams.

Then came a push on both shoulders at once, so quick and jarring she barely had time to brace her legs as she stumbled backward into a chair. Her body smacked against the wood. Her hands grabbed ahold of the arms, feeling the soft grain beneath her fingertips. She knew exactly where she was now. She was in her father's favorite chair by the fire, where he used to sit and tell them made-up stories about four brave and strong princesses who would one day fight a terrifying foe.

Looked like, for her, that day was now.

Her limbs had started to shake, and she didn't try to stop them. Better to let her kidnappers believe she was too scared to think, let alone preparing to fight back.

"Now you're going to tell me where I can find every single scrap of information in this house that can be traced to Vamana Enterprises," the one who'd bellowed at her before barked.

She decided to mentally dub him Loud Voice.

"I have no idea what you're talking about!" she blurted out, which was true. Yes, she was vaguely aware of the mega-company that owned stadiums, restaurants and various other entertainment complexes across the country, including a mammoth one on Toronto's waterfront. But she'd never had the money or inclination to set foot in one. She was vaguely aware from office gossip that the billionaire CEO Franklin Vamana had been fighting off a hostile take-over attempt from his younger sister, Esther, who herself ran a makeup empire called Indigo Iris. But the small legal aid law firm Leia worked at never came anywhere close to representing anyone as big or wealthy as either of them.

"Well, you better start remembering fast," Loud Voice said, "before things get nasty."

Or Leia could just get out of here instead. Faint echoes told her Loud Voice was a few feet in front of her. A creak on the floor-boards and a thudding sound indicated that Stompy Boots was now yanking books off the shelf on the other side of the room. But the one who'd propelled her across the floor wasn't touching her now, which meant there was still one criminal left for her senses to find.

"Tie her to the chair," Loud Voice said, "then come help me search."

A pair of beefy hands grabbed Leia's left wrist. A loop of rope wrapped around it, fastening her to the arm of the chair. So that's where Big Hands was. Leia's jaw set. *All right, time to get out of here.*

Father God, guide me now.

"You have the wrong place!" she insisted. "There's nothing like that here. I promise!"

The rope tightened around her left wrist. Her right hand flew, hammering her fist into the man trying to restrain her before he could even tie the knot. Then she leaped to her feet, even as she heard Big Hands swearing in pain, and grabbed ahold of the chair they'd forced her to sit on and swung it around in front of her like a weapon. The rope fell free. The chair cracked hard against what she hoped was some part of Loud Voice's body before crashing into what she guessed was Big Hands's already throbbing head.

Stunned silence fell, followed by swearing and Loud Voice's command to "Get her!" But it was too late. Leia had already tossed the chair and started running.

She pelted across the living room floor, still thwarted by the blindfold, and guided herself by the smell of the kitchen ahead, the feel of the floorboards beneath her and the sound of the summer rain striking the windows. Her fingers flitted along the books on the shelves until she felt the narrow gap between the third and fourth sets of shelves. She gasped a breath and slid through, pushing her body into the narrow space. A hand reached for her, yanking the fabric of her jacket. She pulled free from the grasp and squeezed into the even smaller space behind the row of shelves. Silent prayers of thanksgiving poured from her lips as she felt for the secret hatch in the wall, crawled through and tumbled into the pitch-black hidden passage behind it. The smell of old dust and fresh soap filled her senses. She shoved the panel closed again, pushing the padlock in place as she did, so no one could follow.

Only then did she stop long enough to finally untie the blindfold and yank it from her face.

A faint light flickered behind her as a warm hand touched her shoulder.

"Hey, Leia."

* * *

As an undercover officer of the Ontario Provincial Police's cold-case homicide division, Jay should've known that Leia's immediate reaction would be to rear around and try to punch anyone who snuck up behind her like that. Or so he thought as he barely managed to duck out of the way of her approaching fist.

She pulled her punch, just before her hand struck the wall in the exact spot his nose had been seconds before. *Impressive.* Instinctively he grabbed her hand before she could draw it back. But instead of pulling away, she grabbed his wrist in return and their hands locked in the grasp like two soldiers, with one trying to haul the other up to safety.

"Nice punch," he said.

Her violet eyes flashed in the dim light of the cell phone that he'd sat in his breast pocket.

"I also just escaped three intruders while blindfolded and partially tied to a chair," she said. Her voice barely rose above a whisper, not that he expected whoever was trashing things on the other side of the wall could hear them.

She hadn't added the words *no thanks to you*, but they seemed to be implied.

"I'm sorry I didn't get here faster," he said. "I was in my camper behind the barn, noticed a light was on and came over. What's going on?"

"You expect me to believe you have no idea what's happening?" Leia demanded. "I don't know what kind of trouble you're messed up in, but there's no other reason I can think of why my family home would be under attack."

What could he possibly say to that? Like everything else he'd said to Leia since he'd first bumped into her in the barn last summer and felt his heart stop, what he'd just told her was entirely true, while leaving out almost everything that he actually wanted to tell her. Now, after over a year of carefully constructed conversations designed to keep from really telling her everything, even as he'd developed very inconvenient feelings for the fiery would-be lawyer, where would he even begin?

It had started with the corpse of a cold-case John Doe that was discovered encased in the cement of a building foundation in downtown Toronto. It had been complete except for a single missing leg bone. The story had of course hit the news and reignited rumors of the "Phantom Killer," who'd been responsible for the disappearance of almost a dozen people over thirty-five years ago. Then came a phone call to the tip line claiming Doe was a waiter who'd been murdered by billionaire CEO Franklin Vamana. The source turned out to be an elderly farmer, Walter Dukes. Walter claimed his late best friend had secretly witnessed the crime and there were more bodies to be found. Franklin had also apparently threatened this best friend that if she ever told anyone he was the Phantom Killer he'd murder both her and her family.

But this friend had taken all the evidence needed to prove Franklin was the killer and hidden it somewhere in Walter's farmhouse. No one in the department had been inclined to take Walter seriously. Who would, really? The Phantom Killer's existence might've never been proven, but that hadn't stopped a wealth of urban legend stories and myths from leaping up around it.

But something about Jay's first conversation with Walter had convinced him that, despite how age had addled his memories, Walter was telling the truth. Walter's tip that this friend had anonymously reported the murder to Toronto police at the time had in fact panned out. An anonymous woman had indeed called the police tip line and left an extended message claiming Franklin was the Phantom Killer. But any investigation into it had been buried through lack of evidence and probably also corruption.

So, Jay had agreed to Walter's suggestion that he move onto the property undercover as a farmhand, while he helped Walter sort through both his muddled memories and belongings for anything this friend had hidden, as well as helping to keep the family safe.

Maybe he'd just wanted to believe Walter's story.

Jay's own mother had gone to her grave insisting that the Phantom Killer had murdered Jay's father, instead of agreeing with the police department's assessment that the recovering alcoholic had just relapsed again and run out on his wife and child. His supervisors hadn't even considered it a serious enough possibility to keep Jay from taking this case.

Developing deep and extremely unauthorized feelings for Leia had been just one of the nails in the coffin of the investigation that his supervisors had considered a wild-goose chase. Even though he'd successfully nipped those emotions in the bud before they'd cost him his career. If Walter had remembered this friend's name, he wasn't about to tell Jay, and nothing even remotely connected to Vamana was ever found. When Walter had died, the operation was called off. Then last week another cold-case John Doe corpse had been found encased in cement, again with one bone missing.

Long story short, I'm trying to determine if one of the wealthiest men in the world is a cold-case serial killer. My only source was your late father, and he passed away insisting there was evidence on this farm.

"I don't know what you want me to say," he admitted.

"Tell me those men didn't just kidnap and blindfold me because of some trouble you're in," she said.

"They didn't," he said. "That much I can promise. Did they say anything?"

"They asked me where to find everything in this house that can be traced to Franklin Vamana."

Jay felt his heart stop in his chest. He'd been meticulously careful to keep the fact he was heading to the Dukes farm tonight need-to-know only. Seemed Walter had been right to worry that if he spoke to police Vamana would somehow find out and send hired mercenaries after his family.

And I promised to protect them.

"What did you say to them?" he asked.

"That they'd come to the wrong place," she said.

He blew out a hard breath. So, despite the fact he'd urged Walter to tell his four daughters the truth before he died, it seemed that he'd stubbornly stuck to his plan to keep them in the dark until the very end. Why would he do that? What could be so terrible in there that he never wanted his daughters to find? He just prayed he found the files before they did. "How many hostiles are we dealing with?"

"Three hostiles that I know of," she said. "All in the living room."

More than he could apprehend himself, at least until he isolated each of them. Also, he couldn't help but notice her lips had quirked at the word *hostiles*, like she was teasing him. So much for worrying she'd figured out he was a cop.

"They took my phone along with my wallet and keys," she added. "Tell me you called the police."

I am the police. Not that he was autho-

rized to tell her that at the risk of compromising the investigation or any evidence it might turn up.

"I don't have a cell phone signal," he admitted.

"Must be the storm," she said. "The tower goes down intermittently when the wind's bad."

"I'll keep checking," he said. Even then, the closest cops were in the small town of Kilpatrick. Backup would take at least an hour to arrive. The question was what to do until then? They couldn't hide in the hidden passage forever. "What do the intruders look like?"

"No idea," she said. "I was blindfolded. But going by handgrip and footsteps, at least two of them are pretty big. They could be dressed up as clowns or wearing gorilla masks for all I know."

Despite himself, he snorted. It was no wonder he'd initially fallen so hard for this woman, before he'd been smart enough to shut those feelings down. Yes, she was impossibly stubborn and strong-willed. But her sense of humor and bravery rivaled that of the best fellow officers he'd served with. There were far worse people to be stuck in a tight spot with, and he'd been in his share of them. Even if she'd never forgive him when she found out the truth.

Now, to find a way out.

"Well, here's hoping it's not clowns," he said. Banging noises rose louder from the other side of the wall, like the intruders were trying to rip the mounted bookshelves clear off the studs. The secret hatch rattled futilely against the padlock. He stepped back and pulled Leia even deeper into the passage. "We've got to get out of here."

"And warn Sally," she said. "She'll be driving up in the morning, unless Mabel wakes up early and she thinks a drive will put her back to sleep."

That much he knew. Sally's estranged husband, Vince, was a mechanic and amateur race-car driver who had a record for drag racing. But besides that, he had been eliminated as a suspect in connection with anything to do with Vamana or the Phantom Killer.

They started down the hidden passage, back the way he'd come. Their shoulders bumped against each other.

"Have you heard of the Phantom Killer?" he asked. "Almost a dozen people disappeared from downtown Toronto when I was a little kid and before you were born. Their bodies were never found."

"Vaguely," she said. "My dad treated anything that happened in the big city like it was a distant and foreign world."

"Rumor is that Franklin Vamana is the killer," he ventured.

"Really?" She sounded genuinely surprised.

"Did you know that before your father married your mother, he had a close friend who worked for Franklin Vamana?" he asked. "A woman. He said she was his best friend and they were so close he once drove through the night to save her life."

"What?" She stopped short. "No, he didn't. Mom and Dad were high school sweethearts, and she was the closest person in the world to him. They were married a few months after graduation, and I showed up just shy of ten months later."

Yes, that was the story Walter had wanted his daughters to believe. Jay still had no idea why.

"That doesn't mean he didn't have another female best friend who he was that close to," he said, "who worked in downtown Toronto at the time."

"I don't know what you're implying," Leia

said. "Or why you're even bringing this up now. But that doesn't make sense. My dad hated all cities and avoided them at all costs. You should've seen how he balked when we tried to talk him into even taking us to Niagara Falls when we were little. He never once mentioned having a friend who lived in Toronto. Let alone a best friend. In fact, Dad was always really opposed to my moving and working there. He was kind of paranoid about stuff like that. I mean, look—he built a house with hidden tunnels in it."

And couldn't she see that was saving her life now?

Just because somebody was paranoid didn't mean that nobody was out to get them.

Forgive me, Lord. Maybe if I'd taken Walter more seriously and pushed a little harder in my investigation we wouldn't be in this situation now.

"What's her name?" she asked. "This secret best friend of my father?"

"He never told me," Jay said. "But he did tell me that she was dead and what she knew about Vamana put you and your sisters' lives in danger. Your father thought your family had enemies."

"My father thought a lot of things," Leia

said. "That didn't mean they were true." She stopped, and he realized they'd reached the hidden door leading outside that he'd used to sneak inside the house. "I get the fact that the criminals in there mentioning Vamana Enterprises is weird, but if this friend existed I've never heard of her. We can talk all that out once we get out of here and call the police. But for now, we've got to make sure Sally and the baby don't drive up early."

He turned off his phone's flashlight. Leia eased the door open a crack and they looked out. Darkness lay on the other side, thick with the smell of summer rain.

The cop in him did a quick calculation. It was essential that he got Leia to safety, warned her sister not to return to the farm and found a way to call in the cavalry to arrest the home invaders before they got away. But could he really risk the criminals getting ahold of the information about Franklin Vamana's crimes that Walter thought were hidden somewhere in the farmhouse?

Especially if he was a cold-case serial killer?

"You go," he said. "Drive as far away from the place as you can, call the police and warn your sister."

"I told you," Leia said, "they took my

keys and I don't have Sally's mechanical knack for hot-wiring cars."

He reached for his keys and heard them jangle in the darkness. "Take my truck. It's in the garage and I've already detached it from my camper."

He tried to press them into her hand, but she pulled her fingers away.

"And just leave you here in danger?" Leia's voice rose. "Are you insane? Look, I don't care how big and strong you are, Jay, there are three of them and one of you. You might not be my favorite person in the world, but I'm not just driving away and leaving you here to die."

The sound of banging and crashing inside the house grew louder. His jaw clenched. There was no time to argue about this now.

"Listen to me," he said. "I'll be fine. You need to go, now."

"Again, I'm not leaving you here to die."

"I'll be fine."

"I don't believe you." She pushed the door open and stepped out into the rain. "And don't tell me Dad would want you to defend the house, because I don't care if they burn it down to the studs."

Even if it meant destroying any chance

of proving a rich and powerful man was the Phantom Killer?

"Leia, listen!" he said. "I'm an undercover cop!"

She turned back and her face paled. "You're what?"

Jay heard the faint click of someone taking the safety off a handgun.

"Leia! Get down!" he shouted as gunfire shattered the night.

TWO

No matter how much time she'd spent with her father and sisters on the range getting used to the explosive sound of gunfire, nothing had prepared her for the way her body froze at the sound of a bullet whizzing past her head.

Then she felt Jay throw his arms around her and pull her into his chest. They hit the ground together and rolled, his body protecting hers like a shield. For a second, they lay there in the wet grass, his panting breath mingling with hers, surrounded by the familiar scents of the man she'd once thought she loved and the falling rain. The sound of bullets ended.

"So, that makes at least four bad guys," she said. "Tell me you're armed, Cop Boy."

"I'm not," he said. "Come on, we've got a second while he reloads."

He eased her out of his arms and grabbed

her hand. They crawled back across the ground to the door and tumbled inside. He slammed it shut and bolted it behind them as a fresh clatter of bullets rang outside, along with what sounded like someone shouting for backup.

"But you really are a cop?" Leia asked.

"Yeah." Jay ran one hand through his damp hair. "Sorry."

"Sorry that you're a cop," she asked, "or that you didn't tell me?"

"Neither," he said. "I'm sorry that my service weapon is locked in the glove compartment of my truck, as per OPP regulations. I saw your car pull up, honestly thought you were the only one in here and didn't stop to get it. Figured the conversation would be tense enough without risking you realizing I was packing. Because, honestly, even if I strapped it to my ankle under my jeans I wouldn't put it past you somehow noticing. Which I now get was a huge mistake on my part. And apparently my second one of the night, as I also somehow missed the arrival of at least four criminals. I actually love being a cop. And while it killed me not to tell you, I'd have been risking my job and investigation if I had."

"But pretending you liked me didn't?"

The words flew out of her mouth before she could bite them back, yet somehow still left a bitter taste in her mouth. This man had held her hand and kissed her. When he'd abruptly called it off and she'd demanded to know why, all he'd said was he was messed up in something he couldn't talk about and then ruefully said if it'd been up to him he'd have married her.

She'd thought he'd meant he'd been flat broke or in some kind of minor trouble with the law.

She'd never guessed he *was* the law.

"It wasn't pretend," Jay said curtly. Like the bitterness on her own tongue infected his, as well. "I more than liked you. But as you can see now, there are way bigger things going on than what two people used to feel for each other. Now, come on."

Used to. Right. Good to know he'd apparently gotten over her just as easily as she'd gotten over him.

He grabbed her hand and turned back toward the hallway as if to lead her somewhere, like this was his childhood home, not hers.

"Hang on." She pulled him back a step. "I still don't actually have a clue what's going on."

"I'm a cop, and bad guys are after us," he said. "That's all you need to know for now."

She dropped his hand and crossed her arms.

"No, it's not," she said. "Now, I get that at last count there were three bad guys in the living room, another one outside and we're trapped in the middle. Plus, the storm's probably cut out your cell phone signal, and you're the big impressive Cop Man—"

"At least that's a step up from Cop Boy—"

Her lips quirked and she almost laughed at that before she caught herself.

"But this is my home and my family we're talking about," she went on, "and I daresay I know both a whole lot better than you. So, if you want us to get out of here alive…"

"Fine," Jay said. "But I'm not arguing with you and you're not going to repeat any of this to anyone."

"Except my three younger sisters—" she interrupted.

"Including Sally, Quinn and Rose." A faint growl rumbled in his voice, mingling with the thunder outside. "As I'm not authorized to tell *you*, I'm not about to give you permission to tell *them*." She didn't answer and guessed he'd taken that as agreement a moment later when he continued. "Last year, the body of a John Doe turned up encased in cement in the foundations of a Toronto office building during construction—"

"Yeah, we covered this—"

"Your dad called the police tip line saying his best friend witnessed Franklin Vamana murder this John Doe over thirty-five years ago—"

"Which I'm not sure I believe—"

Again, he went on like she hadn't spoken.

"*And* that this corpse was one of several bodies hidden around the city, making him a cold-case serial killer," Jay said, "better known as the Phantom Killer."

"And also that this mysterious best friend of my father, who I've never heard of, hid proof of this in the farmhouse," she added. "I'm sorry, I just can't believe it."

Could she? She'd always suspected her father was keeping something from her and her sisters, but this? She shuddered a breath.

"I told you, I'm not about to argue with you," Jay said.

Well, that was easy enough for him to say, she thought. It wasn't his life that had just been tossed inside out. Leia pressed her hand against her solar plexus and tried to calm her heartbeat.

Jay stepped closer to her in the hallway and something softened in his voice. "Look, the way you're feeling right now is perfectly normal, and once we get out of here I'll help connect you with the kind of people who can help you process all this. Thankfully feelings are temporary and don't need to control our actions. Right now, we have to focus on getting out of here safely and warning Sally not to drive up early."

"We agree on that much," she said. After all, her father had taught his four girls how to fight, hunt, shoot, escape danger, forage and survive. Whether she liked it or not, it was like she'd sort of been preparing her entire life for this.

The sound of a rhythmic pounding rose from down the other end of the hallway, like someone was taking a makeshift battering ram to the living room wall. Bullets clanged on their other side against the reinforced door leading outside. It was only a matter of time before somebody found a way in.

"Let's go," Jay said. They ran down the passage and started up a flight of stairs. They'd reached the second floor when she realized she'd let him lead the way. Then again, there wasn't really anywhere else for them to go. He eased the door open to the upstairs hallway. It was empty and so silent she realized just how soundproof the house must be, considering the chaos she knew was happening on the main floor.

The bedroom Quinn and Rose had shared lay to their right, along with the one she'd shared with Sally. Her father's bedroom and study were to the left. Staircases headed back downstairs at opposite ends to the hallway.

But somehow her eyes latched on to the picture straight ahead of her. It was a framed family portrait taken almost a decade ago when she was sixteen. Sally was fourteen and a half and twins Quinn and Rose were twelve. It was a picture that had always irked her. Her sisters were all wide smiles and bouncy hair, all in various shades and waves of honey to taffy blond. And there she was, rail-thin in a blazer and jeans, her jet-black hair falling straight to her shoulders and her violet-eyed gaze piercing the camera. Like someone had cut and pasted her into a family where she didn't quite belong.

Jay paused and shone his cell phone's flashlight on the ceiling above them. The light lingered over a hatch.

"Your dad was convinced that this friend had hidden something in the attic," he said, "and if anything ever went wrong to take you and your sisters there. Not that I could

find anything there but brick walls and cobwebs. It's just a small empty space."

"I wouldn't know," she said. "We were
never allowed up there. He kept the trap door
to the attic locked. I climbed onto the roof
once when I was twelve just to get some
space from my sisters, and he seemed more
upset I might be trying to break into the attic
through the window than that I could fall to
my death if the shingles might tear loose."

Footsteps sounded up the stairs to their
right. They spun to see a short and balding
man, with a wide forehead and narrowed
eyes, dressed in a black shirt and jeans.
"Hey, you!" he yelled.

Loud Voice by the sound of it.

Without even thinking, Leia yanked the
family portrait off the wall and hurled it at
the intruder like a sharp-edged discus. Then
she darted into Rose and Quinn's room, with
Jay one step behind her.

He slammed the door and bolted it shut,
but she stared at it as if seeing it for the first
time. Why did her childhood home have so
many locks on interior doors? For that matter, why did her childhood home have so
many back passages and hidden hatches?
And why had her father insisted on home-

schooling them until high school and run them through so many survival drills?

Help me, Lord. What am I missing?

She'd assumed he was just kooky and maybe paranoid. But she'd loved her father and she'd always trusted him. The idea that he might have been keeping something major from her made her sick to her stomach.

"So, no gorilla masks or clown makeup," Jay said dryly.

"That's Loud Voice," she said. "He's the one who interrogated me."

"You named them?" His cell phone light flickered on again. She turned toward him. Light and shadow moved over his face, highlighting the strong lines of his jaw. He was grinning.

"Know thy enemy," she said. "I called the other two that were in the living room Stompy Boots and Big Hands."

He chuckled. It was a warm and deep sound that seemed to fill the space.

"The good and bad news is that I recognize Loud Voice from mug shots I've collected of Canada's Most Wanted," Jay said. "He's a goon for hire who goes by a lot of different aliases, according to his rap sheet. Stan Austin, Bradley Smith and Martin Lee are the main ones, but off the top of my head I can't remember which is his real name."

"Stan works," she said. "You dealt with him before?"

"Not personally," he said, "and if I do my job right as an undercover cop, he'll never know I exist. My goal is to spend my life as a nameless, faceless detective taking down guys like him. I've literally built an actual crime wall full of pictures of criminals I hope to catch one day, and he's on it. Maybe some of the other guys here are, too. Vamana is powerful and connected enough to hire a bunch of thugs."

His brown eyes darkened in the dim light and something seemed to stretch and tighten in the air between them like an elastic band waiting to snap.

"But are you okay?" he asked softly.

"Of course," she said lightly. "Who wouldn't be?"

She tried to smile, but for some inexplicable reason something about both the sound of his voice and the tenderness of his touch sent unexpected tears to her eyes. She blinked them back hard. No, she was not about to fall apart now. She turned back toward the room. It was wide, with a single big window and twin beds nestled on opposite sides of the room. She grabbed for Rose's old pink princess phone on the table beside her bed and held the receiver to her ear. No dial tone. She pushed the receiver button up and down, then traced the cord around the wall to make sure it was plugged in.

"Phone's dead," she said. "Guessing they cut the phone lines."

He blew out a hard breath and cast a glance at his phone again. "No cell, either."

She looked to where rain beat almost invisibly against the pitch-black pane. "Normally you can see the light of the cell tower blinking from here."

Silence had fallen on the other side of the locked door, but somehow she doubted that was a good thing. She dropped to one knee beside Quinn's bed, reached into the mattress boards and felt around for the thick rope and smooth wooden rungs of the ladder her sister had used to sneak in past curfew. It was still there. She pulled it out. "Well, thankfully we've got more than one way out of this room."

Jay's face paled slightly and she suddenly remembered from last summer that heights were his biggest fear—specifically falling from them—thanks to a minor inner-ear issue he'd been born with.

"Don't worry," she added. "Quinn used it

to climb out the window past curfew all the time as a teen. She was the rebellious one."

Jay blew out a long breath.

"What will we do if your dad was right and there's some evidence of Vamana's crimes hidden somewhere in the house?" he asked. "This might be our last chance to find it before it's either stolen or destroyed."

"I know," she said, "and to be clear, Stan never said what kind of information about Vamana Enterprises they're here looking for. But I'm guessing it's not old concert tickets. This is all new to me. I have no idea what could even be here or where it might be hidden. Right now, the only thing I can worry about is warning Sally. But that doesn't mean that what you're looking for is not important, too."

Even though this was the first she was hearing about it and still wasn't sure what to believe.

"Okay, how about this as a strategy?" she added. "What if we split up? I can create a distraction and draw them away from the house, while you do a very fast final search. Then if you can't find anything, we run."

"Absolutely not," Jay said. "I'm not using you as a decoy."

"I can climb," she said, "and we're surrounded by forest. There's also the barn and garage. I know you're not a big fan of heights, but climbing these trees and buildings is second nature to me. It's so dark out there they'll never see me up a tree or on a roof in this darkness. I'm not quite as good as Quinn, who does it professionally, but I've free-climbed with her and can definitely hold my own."

"I comprehend what you're saying." Jay's arms crossed over his chest. "But I'm telling you it's not going to happen."

"Look," she said, "I get that you're a cop—"

"I'm also somebody who used to care about you—" Jay's voice rose "—and doesn't want to see you hurt!"

Thunder roared closer and lightning cracked, filling the room in a sudden flash of light. She watched as Jay's face suddenly paled as he looked past her. The room fell dark again.

"It's…it's gone," he stammered.

"What's gone?" she asked.

"The entire cell phone tower," he said. "The cell signal's not just out. The tower's been completely destroyed."

"What do you mean by *destroyed*?" Leia

asked, and something ached in his chest at the fear in her voice. Her white-knuckled fingers still gripped the rope ladder like she'd almost forgotten she was holding it.

"It's like…" Words failed him as he tried to think of a way to describe the twisted wreck of metal he'd seen bent toward the ground. "It's like someone literally fastened their vehicle to the cell tower and physically pulled it down."

Which meant they'd premeditated their attack. He stood there and silently prayed as he watched Leia process the news. Why hadn't he stepped up and tried to reach out to her sooner? He'd stepped over a line when he'd let his heart be so drawn to her and created that kind of close emotional connection that wasn't just ill-advised but could cost him both this case and his career.

She'd never know that losing her had split his heart open, too, and made him feel like a piece of it was missing.

"Then what's the plan, Cop Man?" Leia asked. She paced the room like a tiger in a cage. "We can't stay trapped in here forever. Running around the house battling thugs for hire could get us killed, and someone intentionally took out both the phone line and cell tower. That just leaves climbing out the window, getting in your truck and driving away. And I do mean driving, because the closest neighbors are at least two hours away on foot and while that's not that far in the grand scheme of things that's a long time to wait before warning Sally and calling in reinforcements."

The muffled sound of voices came from behind the door. He held a finger to his mouth as he crossed to the door and looked out the peephole. Stan was standing outside the door. He was arguing with another, even larger man with a big bruise on his cheekbone and a scowl Jay recognized from his crime wall.

Leia brushed against his shoulder, and he let her look out.

"Pretty sure that's Big Hands," she said. "He's the one who tried to tie me down."

"Looks like you hit him pretty good," he said.

"Recognize him?"

"Yup."

"He got a name?"

"Several," Jay said. "Let's go with Ross Stevil, former military helicopter pilot who got into crime after he was dishonorably discharged for assault, torture and theft."

"Such basic names for such evil people," she said.

Leia stepped away from the peephole. Jay looked back out. Stan was telling Ross to guard the door and he'd be back in a minute with something. Jay didn't want to know what the man was going to get.

Leia crouched beside the window and latched first one side of the rope ladder and then the other to what looked like screws hidden under the frame. "Now can we run?"

He gritted his teeth and didn't answer for a moment.

Lord, help me be wise. Let my brain rule over my foolish heart.

"You go," he said. "Get in my truck, drive until you get a cell phone signal and call for help."

To his shock, she actually snorted.

"No," she said. "Believe it or not, I actually care about you, too. If I'm not allowed to hide in a tree because you're too worried about my safety, then I'm definitely not about to just leave you stranded here alone in a farmhouse with baddies."

"Leia, it's my job—" he started.

"To try to take down four armed criminals all by yourself without backup?" she interrupted. "Don't forget, I work for legal aid and I'm in law school. I might not be a cop, but I know well enough to realize that you're completely within your rights to run with me right now and keep yourself safe. Plus, I'm a civilian, and you've got an obligation to protect me."

He gritted his teeth and resisted the urge to point out that her plan was far more dangerous than his. She wasn't entirely wrong. He was outnumbered, and going for backup was protocol, as was protecting her.

But could he really get this close to proving once and for all if Franklin Vamana was the Phantom Killer?

His mother's belief that the Phantom Killer was the real reason his father had disappeared might turn out to be no more than her way of dealing with the loss. But still, Jay knew at a young age what it was like to have someone he loved hug him goodbye, promise he'd see him later and never return.

The distraught mess his mother had fallen into had been what had made Jay teach himself how to switch off unwanted emotions. He didn't let himself feel and definitely never let anyone get so close that losing them could destroy him. It was how he'd shut down his unfortunate feelings for Leia and a skill that would help make him the kind of undercover detective he wanted to be.

But if there was any possibility that there was evidence in this house that would help him bring peace to the families of the Phantom Killer's victims, how could he just let it go?

The noise on the other side of the door grew louder. He looked out the peephole: they were using a crowbar to tear off the hinges.

"They're breaking in," he said.

"Then I'm going now, and you're coming with me," Leia said. She turned back to the window and slid it open. Rain and wind whipped in toward them. She threw the ladder outside and then slid her body through. "I'd better see you down there."

"Wait," he started. "I don't know if there really is any information about the Phantom Killer hidden in this farmhouse. But I think before we escape I have to at least try to do something to save it."

He couldn't just run and let Vamana's hired goons find and destroy the evidence. There had to be another way. Even if he couldn't see it for the life of him right now.

But before he could say anything more, she disappeared through the window and was gone.

THREE

"Leia!" Jay leaned his body out the window and whispered her name as loudly as he dared. He watched Leia climb down the thin rope ladder into the wind and rain as it shook and twisted beneath her. She was navigating it so smoothly she might've been strolling across a sunny lawn. She was absolutely incredible and impossible in equal amounts. "Just give me one moment and don't go anywhere without me. I'm right behind you."

The sound of intruders trying to wrench the door open grew louder. He didn't exactly like the fact they'd actually stopped to plan how to break in instead of just barging in. It meant they were thinking, planning and probably answerable to someone on the outside world who was giving them orders. Or maybe they'd already tried to break another door down and realized just how reinforced they were. It was undeniable that Walter had built his farmhouse into a protective fortress. Jay just didn't know why.

Franklin Vamana had very deep pockets and could definitely afford to hire professional criminals to do his dirty work.

Or am I wrong, Lord? There's still so much I just don't understand. Including the fact Leia didn't believe Walter's story about this nameless best friend. And now, by running with her, Jay was about to give up any hope of finding whatever this friend, who may or may not have even existed, had hid. *Help me, Lord.*

He threw his shoulder into an antique dresser and slowly shoved it across the door, praying with each step. It wouldn't buy them a lot of time, but it would some. Then he ran for the window and looked out. Leia was nowhere to be seen. He gritted his teeth, slid his body through and climbed down. His hands and feet slipped as the wooden rungs spun beneath his weight. He reached the bottom and stared out into the empty night.

A hand grabbed his arm and he spun, his hands raised to fight.

"Easy there, Cop Boy," Leia whispered. "It's just me."

Relief flooded his core as he felt her hand grab his.

"I thought you'd taken off without me," he said.

"Nope." Her fingers tightened their squeeze. "You know where your gun's hidden, and I'm still hoping that before this is all over you'll let me shoot it. As you'll remember, I did beat you on the range once. Which I now feel even more impressed by considering you're a cop."

"Yes, I remember you're a great shot," he said. "And no, you're not shooting my gun."

Despite himself, he felt his lips twitch in a reflexive grin. There was just something about her sense of humor that got to him in a way nobody else's ever had before. Everything about her got under his skin, for that matter, in both good and bad ways. If he was honest, he'd kind of missed her.

He took a deep breath and reminded himself that he couldn't afford to revisit the emotions she once stirred in him. He pulled his hand from hers.

"So, what's the plan?" she asked.

"Hopefully nobody knows we've escaped the house," he said. "I say we run for the tree line and then circle back around the farm until we reach the garage, using the trees as cover. Then we hop in my truck and get out of here."

It went without saying that he'd be the one driving and the one shooting, if need be.

"Sounds good to me," she said.

They ran through the rain, across the damp grass, until they reached the trees. Then they picked their way through the brambles and branches in silence until they reached the garage. There he paused, feeling Leia come to a stop one step behind him. The farmhouse was to their left now and the garage to his right. A slender man, perhaps the same one who'd fired at them earlier, strode back and forth between the two buildings swinging a flashlight.

"Recognize him?" she asked.

"Not in this light," Jay said, "but my guess is he's younger and less experienced to get stuck on rain patrol duty. He's probably the guy who shot at us earlier, and I expect he's armed. Now, you stay hidden while I lure him around to this side of the garage, then I'll disarm him and tie him up while you get to the truck."

He paused and waited for her to argue. But she didn't.

"Got it," she said.

And that's when it hit him: despite everything, she still trusted him. Even though his own mind was still scrambling for ways to do this without her. Maybe he'd drive away with her until they were in cell phone range, then get out and run back through the woods while she carried on. Or maybe he'd drop her off somewhere and then return. He wasn't sure yet. All he knew was that once he got her to safety, Leia's part in this whole thing would be over and he'd be carrying on without her.

"If anything happens," he said, "and it's a matter of saving your life or helping me, I want you to do whatever it takes to survive, okay? Don't come back for me. Don't try to rescue me. If push comes to shove, I can handle hiding in the farmhouse with a few masked men until law enforcement arrives. I promise. I've survived worse."

"I don't doubt it," she said, again with that same light, almost teasing tone in her voice that somehow made him feel stronger than what his problems were. "And you can tell me all about it sometime when we're out of here and somewhere safe."

"Just promise me you won't tell anyone I'm a cop," he said, "unless your life is on the line. My ability to stay undercover means everything to me and without it I can't keep investigating crimes this way."

"I won't," she said. "I promise."

He stepped toward her in the darkness and only realized how close they were standing when his arm bumped hers. All it would've taken was for them to turn toward each other and tilt their heads just a little, and their lips would've touched again just like they had before in the rain in these very woods.

Lord, I worked so hard to shut down my feelings for this woman. Please don't let them distract me now. Help me be stronger than my heart.

"Now I'm going to go get the bad guy," he said, his own voice sounding vaguely husky. "I'll signal you when to come out of hiding and join me."

He steeled a breath, then turned and sprinted across the clearing to the side of the garage. Within an instant, he saw movement to his right out of the corner of his eye. The young man with the flashlight was running at him. So far, so good. Jay darted around the side of the garage, pressed himself against the far wall, just out of range of a dim pool of light shining from the window, and prayed. He didn't have long to wait.

The man appeared around the corner. In one quick, smooth and virtually painless motion, Jay brought him down to the ground and pinned him there before he'd even known what hit him. He was young, probably not much more than twenty, with brown curls plastered around his face. Good news was he looked pretty new to criminal enterprise.

Bad news was that Jay couldn't see the man's gun anywhere.

"Hey, I don't know what's going on here," Jay said, keeping his voice low and unthreatening, "and I don't want trouble. I just want to get in my truck and leave." In fact, he was praying very hard he'd be able to resolve this peacefully and without having to use force. Then later, or another day, some other cop would find this man and arrest him. "Where's your gun?"

"I don't have one!" The young man's voice rose.

"But you shot at us, didn't you?" Jay demanded.

"Yeah, but then Stan got mad about that and took it back!" he wailed. "He said I'm not supposed to kill the girl, just be the lookout."

Huh, so this guy was so wet behind the ears that nobody had explained to him how to get ahold of his own illegal gun in Canada. Hopefully the fact they weren't actually trying to kill "the girl" boded well for escaping.

"I'm Jay," he said. "I was hired to tidy this farm up for sale. Do you have a name?"

"Ben."

No last name, but it was a conversation at least.

"What are you doing here, Ben?" he asked.

"You're not a cop, right?" Ben asked. "If so, you've got to tell me."

No, actually, he didn't under Canadian law. Plus, this man wasn't under arrest.

"Do you want me to call the cops?" Jay asked.

No answer.

"Do you work for Vamana?" Jay tried again.

The young man's worried look told him all he needed to know.

"Look, it's not what you think," the young man said. "We're not doing anything wrong. This woman stole something really important from Franklin Vamana. My boss doesn't want the police involved and so sent us to get it from her. Nobody is supposed to get hurt."

Jay sighed. *Oh, Ben, you're being set up as their fall guy if something goes wrong, aren't you?*

"I don't know what she stole," Ben added, "but there's a big reward for bringing her in. Like huge. If you help me, I could split it with you? I've got a new baby, and his mama won't let me see him again until I sort out some legal problems."

So Ben was both naive and foolish, Jay thought. He hoped the young man was arrested and through that got the help he needed before he got himself killed.

"Do you know the woman's name?" he asked.

"Ann-Margret," Ben said. "This is the Herber farm, right? Ann-Margret Herber?"

Jay blinked. *Who?* Was that the name of Walter's secret friend?

"Honestly," Jay said. "I've never heard of her."

Leia's heart was beating so hard she was sure that Jay and the man he'd pinned could hear it. Sure, she'd heard Jay when he'd told her that he was an undercover cop and it's not that she hadn't believed him. But somehow it felt like an entirely different thing altogether to watch the precision with which he'd first tracked and then taken down his foe. It'd been both impressive and scary. And made everything feel all too real.

"You have the wrong place!" Jay's voice rose, and for the first time she was able to catch anything either of them were saying. "There's nobody here by that name!"

Her heart stopped. Was Jay trying to throw the men off their scent? Or had they really just come to the wrong place and were looking for the wrong person? Maybe there really was no big conspiracy involving her family; maybe her father's memories were muddled and there was no evidence linked to some serial killer hidden in her childhood home. And yet, as she tried to silently thank God for the hope of that, she felt doubt rising within her, as if a whole box of the questions that had been opened in her mind back at the farmhouse just couldn't be ignored.

She may have never heard of Dad's former best friend or some connection between her family and Vamana Enterprises, let alone the Phantom Killer. But for as long as she could remember, her father had lived in fear that someone or something would one day come for his children. She almost believed that he was right.

Twin headlights pierced the darkness

ahead. A car was coming down the long and twisting country road toward them. Jay's head snapped to the approaching vehicle and then his eyes met hers through the darkness as rain streamed down the lines of his face.

She could read in a glance that he was thinking the same thing she was.

Were Sally and the baby back early?

"Go!" Jay called. "Warn them! I'll be two steps behind you. I promise."

She ran without stopping to ask herself whether or not she believed him. Her sister and baby niece could be in danger. That was all that mattered. Voices shouted behind her, but she didn't turn to look and see where they were coming from. Prayers filled her heart as her feet pounded through the trees. She hoped against hope that Jay really would be right behind her and they wouldn't have to leave without him.

The car drew closer. Its bright headlights blinded her eyes. She waved both hands above her head and it skidded to a stop on the muddy road beside her. The passenger's side door flew open in front of her.

It wasn't her sister's car.

"Miss Dukes!" A voice, male and vaguely familiar, cut through the rain. "It's Miss Dukes, right?"

She bent down and looked inside the car. A familiar-looking and heavyset man, probably in his sixties, with thinning hair and a generous nose, leaned across the front seat toward her. It was a local farmer and a friendly acquaintance of her father's, who'd introduced him to her at the farmers market last summer. They'd made small talk there a couple of times and he'd come up to her at her father's funeral to express his condolences. But she hadn't thought he and her father were friends. Dad had always been skeptical of letting anyone get too close. It was a wonder he'd trusted Jay.

"Mr...." Leia searched her mind a beat and came up with a name. "Mr. Dunlop, right?"

"Yes!" His smile was wide and missing part of a tooth. "I didn't know if you'd remember me. What are you doing running around in the wet without an umbrella?" He patted the passenger's seat as rivulets of water streamed down its sides. "You're soaked to the bone. Get in."

She paused for a moment, standing in the rain, battling the voice in her head that told her not to trust anyone. It sounded too much like her father for her liking. Then again, her father was paranoid and had kept her in the dark. She sat, keeping one leg outside of the car in the mud, while the roof sheltered her from the pounding rain outside. Her eyes searched the darkness.

Where are you, Jay?

"What are you doing here so late at night?" she asked.

"The cell tower on your property is down," Mr. Dunlop said. "It took out the signal for the whole block. I wasn't sure if anyone was even on the property, but I came to see if there was anything I could do to help, just in case. Are you living here now? Or one of your sisters?"

"No," she said. "But do you remember that my dad had a farmhand last year named Jay? He's staying here. I'm not going anywhere without him."

Again, her eyes searched the storm, hoping, waiting and even willing him to appear.

"Is there something wrong?" The elderly farmer's voice cut through her mind.

"No," she said. "I mean, yes. The farm has been broken into tonight. Thieves are still there right now. Once Jay gets here we have to drive until we get a signal and call the police."

There, that was as much truth as she'd tell him.

"We should go now," Dunlop said. "You should put your seat belt on."

He reached over, put the car in Reverse and began to back up.

"No!" Leia said, and instinctively yanked her leg inside. "Not without Jay!"

Dunlop hit the brakes so quickly her door slammed shut, almost clipping her knee.

"Listen, Miss Dukes." Dunlop's voice sharpened. He yanked a badge from his coat pocket. "I'm an undercover police officer. I retired a few years ago, but came out of retirement to help keep an eye on your father. We have reason to believe that a friend of his entrusted him with some vital property belonging to Vamana Enterprises. Vamana wants it back."

Her heart stopped painfully as if it had gotten snagged somewhere inside her.

Did that mean he was working with Jay? If so, why hadn't Jay told her? Did Dunlop even know another cop was stationed here?

But Jay had made her promise not to blow his cover, no matter what.

"I have no idea about anything related to Vamana," she said, which was the truth. "But when Jay gets here we can talk all that out."

Something rustled in the trees and then

a dark shape loomed ahead of them in the headlights, running toward them. Even in silhouette, Jay's broad shoulders and strong form was unmistakable. Relief cascaded over her. *Thank You, God!* "And that's Jay now!"

She reached for the door to open it and call out to him. The lock clicked. Dunlop put the car in Drive.

"Stop!" Her hand darted out and reflexively grabbed the steering wheel. "I'm not going anywhere without Jay!"

"Yes, you are, Miss Dukes," Dunlop said. His voice was flat and emotionless, verging on cold. He reached into his side door, pulled out a small black canister of pepper spray and aimed it at her. Then, for good measure, he pulled his coat back enough to show off his gun. "I'm not going to kill you, I promise. I don't even want to hurt you. I just need you to cooperate and come quietly, without fuss. I'm only going to take you somewhere quiet and you're going to tell me everything you know about Vamana and the Phantom Killer."

FOUR

Jay ran through the rain, pelting helplessly after the car even as it turned around in a tight circle on the muddy ground and then drove off down the narrow lane. Dread filled his core. It wasn't Sally's car and somehow he knew that Leia would have never voluntarily leaped into a vehicle and left without him. Someone unknown was kidnapping her and taking her somewhere, and there was nothing he could do to stop it.

Still he ran, chasing after the car as the headlights grew smaller and smaller in the distance, until finally he lost sight of it in the trees. Only then did he stop running, but even then he kept jogging slowly through the rain as if she might reappear.

It was too late. He'd taken too long questioning Ben and then leaving him tied up under an overhang out of the rain. Then Jay had sprinted for his truck and stuck the key in the ignition, only to find the engine wouldn't turn over. Thankfully his gun had still been in the glove compartment and was now in his ankle holster. But that was cold comfort. The truck was sabotaged, Leia had been taken and he hadn't been able to save her, leaving him helpless to do anything but pray.

This is all my fault. Help her, Lord. Save her. Keep her safe.

But still he kept moving, pushing his body through the storm into the darkness as the rain beat against his head.

Suddenly the sound of a blaring horn overtook the air. Then came the sound of brakes squealing and the deafening screech of metal crashing, seeming to shake the forest around them. Then it faded, leaving nothing but red flashing lights and the plaintive wail of someone or something leaning on a car horn.

Leia! He sprinted toward the sound of the wreck. The trees seemed to glow on and off ahead of him. Then he saw the car mangled and mashed against a tree but still upright. An overweight man climbed out of the driver's seat and stumbled down the road with a gun in his hand. The man froze in the blinking lights as if suddenly realizing Jay was there. The weapon raised in his hand.

But Jay wasn't about to give him time to decide to fire. He ran straight at the man, counting on the element of surprise, the storm around him, his own police training and God's help to help him survive. Jay leaped and tackled him to the ground, just as he fired. The bullet whizzed into the trees somewhere beyond them. The man swung, catching Jay in the jaw just hard enough to get him to relinquish his grip, before slithering from his grasp and taking off into the woods.

Jay let him go and ran for the car, just in time to see the passenger's door open and Leia tumble out and onto the ground.

"Leia!" he called. His heart leaped in relief. "Are you okay?"

They had to run. Any moment now her kidnapper could be back and with company. But Leia whimpered in pain. Her hands cradled her face, and in a moment the thick and pungent smell coming through the open car door told him why.

Leia had been pepper-sprayed.

In two seconds, he'd reached her and crouched down by her side.

"We've got to move," he said. "Take my hand and I'll lead you."

She turned to him. Her eyes were swollen and shut. Tears streamed down her face, mingling with the rain.

"Jay!" She practically crawled into his arms as his name slipped from her lips in a sob. "He wanted to know about Vamana and threatened me with a gun. But I didn't break your cover."

His heart ached so much it pained him to breathe.

"Hey, it's okay," he said. "I'm here and I'm going to get you out of this. You were hit with pepper spray?"

"Yeah," she whimpered, "it hurts, and I can't see."

He held her tightly, cradled her to his chest as he stood and guided her up to her feet.

"I've heard it hurts a lot," he said. "I've been caught in my fair share of pepper spray, but I've never taken a hit directly to the face like that, so I can only imagine. But your kidnapper has run off with his gun and I expect either he'll be back or somebody else will be, so we've got to move."

He led her away from the car.

"Dunlop," she said. "That's what his name was."

"Jim or James?" he asked. He hadn't recognized the man in the darkness but he definitely knew the name.

"Maybe," she said. "Big nose, heavy guy, said he was a retired cop. My dad knew him from the farmers market and he came to my dad's funeral."

He blew out a breath. "Yeah, I think I know him. I'll show you his mug shot later. He was a cop, but a corrupt one who was discharged and I guess is now for hire."

But at least it was a lead.

Voices rose from the darkness. Flashlight beams swung through the trees.

"Someone's coming," he said urgently. Several someones, in fact, by the sound of it. He slid his arm around her waist. "Can you run? Or should I carry you?"

"I can run," she said. Her chin rose. "I just can't see."

"Well, he did get you pretty good."

"He didn't do it," she said. "I did."

He wasn't sure what she meant by that and didn't have time to ask. The voices were getting louder, combined with the crunching and cracking sounds of people coming through the trees. There was no time to run, only hide. A thick and fallen tree, heavy with moss and branches, lay to their right, still leaning on its stump.

"Get down," he said, his voice so low he wasn't even sure if she'd heard him. But she didn't resist as he pulled her to the ground, wrapped his arms around her and rolled under the fallen tree.

They stopped and lay there for a moment, side by side on their stomachs, on the muddy ground, listening to the rain beating on the fallen tree as it sheltered them from above. The warmth of her body was pressed against his side and, when she spoke, her voice was a rugged gasp in his ear.

"What happened to the guy you jumped?" she whispered.

"Tied him up, took his knife and left him somewhere safe," he whispered back.

"Where's your truck?"

"Someone disabled it."

"Got your gun?" she asked.

"Yeah, but I'm still not letting you shoot it, especially as you can't see."

She laughed softly through her tears and the sound was music to his ears. They lapsed back into silence. For a while he didn't hear anything but the muffled and chaotic sounds of voices and people running through the trees.

Then a single male voice bellowed above the noise. "Where is she?"

"That's Stan," she whispered. "I think he's in charge here, but he's not the big boss."

"I don't know!" another voice replied. "I left her in the car, alive and with a face full of pepper spray!"

"That's Dunlop," she whispered.

A loud and furious barrage of swear words filled the air, punctuated by death threats. Jay counted four figures in total, most of whom were now yelling profanities. It seemed Stan was angry that Leia was missing. Dunlop was yelling back that it wasn't his fault. The other two men on the team were taking opposite sides. Looked like no one had found and freed Ben yet. Jay's heart pounded. The smell of damp earth filled his lungs. He reached for Leia's hand and squeezed it.

It wouldn't be long until the criminals stopped infighting and started searching.

"The boss wants the woman taken alive!" Dunlop shouted.

"Not that one!" Stan barked.

"How do you know she can't lead us to her?"

"Who are they after?" Leia's voice was in his ear.

"Don't just stand there!" Stan shouted before he could answer. "Find her!"

Jay's limbs tensed to run. He pulled himself up onto the balls of his feet like a sprinter ready to bolt.

"What was she doing in your car?" Stan shouted. A chill cut through his voice.

"I wanted to question her!" Dunlop yelled.

"You wanted all the money for yourself!"

Lightning flashed, swamping the forest in light. Instinctively, Jay glanced up. The two criminals were standing face-to-face beside the car. Each one clutched a gun in their hands. Darkness fell again as the lightning faded, followed by the sound of a gunshot and a flash of light.

As Jay's eyes adjusted to the night again, he watched as Dunlop fell to the ground; he'd been shot dead.

The sound of the gunshot rang in Leia's ears. Fear poured down her spine and she pressed her lips together to keep from crying out. Between the stinging pain in her eyes, the tears still coursing down her face and the storm around her, she still couldn't see a thing. But as she reached for Jay she could feel the strength of his arm under her fingertips. He took her hand and held it.

"Come on," he said. "We have to run while they're distracted."

"Now?" she gasped.

The ring of the gunshot was fading and being overtaken by the sound of people shouting.

"Their leader just killed one of the team in front of them," Jay said. He slid out from under the log and pulled her after him. "It's terrible but we've got to go while they're distracted. It's our only hope."

"I can't see," she said.

"I know," he said. "You're going to have to trust me."

"Where are we going?"

"Back to the farm," he said. "Somewhere we can hide and regroup."

He led her across the ground slowly, both of them staying low and crouching on the balls of their toes. Then he pulled her to her feet and they started running. Voices shouted behind them, but Jay didn't even falter. She gripped his hand tightly and prayed.

Help us, Lord. I'm literally running blind.

There'd been something tentative, almost hesitant, about the Jay who she'd developed feelings for last summer. Yes, he'd seemed so happy to see her every time they snuck away for a walk in the woods or long chat in the dilapidated barn he was repairing. His grin had been infectious, and his dark eyes had shone in a way she didn't even know eyes could come to life. Yet, for all the hours they'd spent together and despite the furtive kisses he'd brushed across her lips, there'd always been something holding him back. She'd always known somehow that he was keeping something from her. But the man now leading her through the woods in the darkness was someone entirely different. This Jay was confident and self-assured. He was protective. And somehow she trusted him even more than she had when she'd thought his heart might be hers.

He stopped so suddenly she would've collided into him if he hadn't reached out his other hand to catch her. Jay pulled her to his side and silently pressed a finger to her lips. She froze, snuggled against his chest and feeling the thud of his heartbeat moving through her. Another bullet cracked through the air, the noise seeming to come from all directions at once. Then Jay squeezed her hand firmly, led her away from the tree and they started running again.

Branches beat against her body. Roots and fallen branches snared her feet.

"Listen," he said. "I'm going to pick you up and carry you."

She shook her head. "No, you don't have to. I'm fine."

"We're about to reach a fairly open patch of ground that's being patrolled and the thieves are getting trigger-happy," he said. "My impression is that they're all in it for the money and there's really no honor among thieves. It'll be easiest if I carried you."

"I'd rather run on my own two feet," she said, "and I know this farm better than anyone."

"I know," he said. "But you're hurt and can't see. Please don't take this the wrong way but I'd pick up and carry anyone in your situation—a witness, a fellow officer, even a bad guy. We pick each other up all the time in basic training. It's not personal."

He sounded indignant, almost like she'd insulted him somehow.

"Got it," she said. She slid her hands up his arms and onto his shoulders. Her fingers gripped his shoulders. He might be about to carry her, but she wasn't going to let him just sweep her up into his arms. "Ready?"

"Yup," he said.

Now she could hear something like laughter in his voice. She jumped and he caught her, looping his arms smoothly under her legs and pulling her to his chest so effortlessly it was like he'd been waiting for her. She wrapped both arms around his neck.

"Don't let go," he said.

Suddenly he was off running again. He sprinted through the forest faster than before, scrambling down slopes and leaping over unseen obstacles. She could hear tree branches breaking against Jay's strong body. The sound of voices rose and fell around them.

"Are they chasing us?" she asked.

"They're trying to," he said. "But don't worry. I won't let them get you. Now, hold on tight."

"I already am!"

"Then hold on tighter!" He spun around quickly, and she felt her body jolt down half an inch as he pulled his right arm out from under her legs. "And if you can, cover your ears."

She buried her face deeper into his neck. She felt him bend down, pull his gun and fire. Then, in an instant, he holstered his weapon and his arm was back under her legs again, supporting her with his strength.

"Sorry about that," he called.

"Tell me you didn't just shoot someone," she said.

"I didn't shoot someone," Jay said. "I shot near enough to someone that they got confused, and it bought us a moment of time. I didn't want to risk them seeing where we were going."

"And where are we going?" she asked.

She knew every corner of her childhood farm like the back of her hand.

"The barn," he said.

The dilapidated building that he'd started working on last summer? The place they used to meet to talk without the family finding out about their relationship?

"No," she said. "It's not secure."

"It is now," he said.

He dropped one hand from her legs again and she heard the old familiar creak of the barn door opening. They stepped inside out of the rain. The smell of hay filled her senses. She opened her eyes, but saw nothing but indistinct blurs, shapes and shadows.

Jay leaped up slightly, and she heard a latch open.

"I reinforced the loft," he said. "It's warm, it's secure and, most importantly, there's something inside that I want you to see. Now I'm going to lift you up."

She reached up and felt the soft wooden ledge of floorboards beneath her fingertips. Instinctively, she heaved herself up through the hatch and into the loft. She pulled herself up to sitting, slid back to make room for Jay and felt a soft, rag-rug carpet under her fingertips.

He hoisted himself up through the hole, closed the hatch behind them and locked it.

"I thought you hated heights," she said, "or did you just tell me that to keep me from coming up here?"

"No, I really do get vertigo," Jay said. "Really was born with an inner-ear problem and can't hear as good out of my left ear as my right. Your eyes keep fluttering open. Can you see?"

"Not much," she admitted, "and they still really hurt."

"Well, there are a couple of giant pillows behind you," he said. "Make yourself comfortable and I'll get you something for your eyes. There's also a cot if you want to nap and some basic food if you're hungry."

The giant pillows weren't much more than large puffy shapes, but they were soft under her touch. She propped one up against the wall and leaned against it. They were surprisingly comfortable.

"So you built a secret hideaway room in the loft of the old barn?" she asked.

And here she'd told him that she and Sally had done the same thing when they were twelve and fourteen to escape their younger sisters. Not that it was this comfortable.

"Pretty much," Jay said.

"But I thought you lived in the camper," she said.

"I do," he said. "But I needed somewhere secure to make calls and map out all my information about the Phantom Killer case. I'll show you everything once your eyes are a bit better. And then we'll figure out where we go from here. The good news is that your sister Sally hasn't come back early and the farm's still standing. Nothing's changed. We just need to find a way to warn your sister, call my colleagues and escape the farm."

"Is that all?" She closed her eyes, leaned back and let her body sink into the pillow, suddenly feeling weary. "I heard the criminals arguing that I wasn't even the woman they were looking for and you told the guy who you jumped outside the garage that he had the wrong place. What happened to him again?"

"I gently tied him up and left him somewhere dry," Jay said. "And he said they were here looking for a woman who'd stolen something important from Vamana Enterprises, someone named Ann-Margret Herber."

Leia sat up sharply, her heart suddenly pounding as if it was trying to escape her chest.

"She was my mother."

FIVE

For a moment she just sat in stunned silence. Her mother was the "friend" of her father who'd seen Franklin Vamana kill someone? It answered all the confusing questions she had, while opening so many more to be answered.

"I thought your mother's name was Annie," Jay said. His voice was gentle as he crouched beside her.

"It was," she said slowly. "But Ann-Margret was her legal name, the one she was born with. Everyone who knew and loved her called her Annie. So when she married my dad, she didn't just change her last name, but decided to use her nickname for her first name while she was at it. At least, that's what my dad told me."

Her voice trailed off.

Jay hesitated for a moment, and even with

her eyes closed she could tell he was there almost hovering beside her.

"I want to get you something for your eyes," he said. "But not until I know you're okay."

She took in a deep breath and let it out slowly.

Lord, help me see what I need to see. Open my eyes to the truth.

"I'm okay," she said. "Thank you. In a way, this makes more sense, and I'm relieved that something finally does."

"So, you think your mom is who your dad was trying to tell me about?" Jay asked.

She felt him move away from her slowly and get up.

"My gut says yes," she said. "It's the only thing that makes any sense at all. My mom was my dad's best friend. She died of cancer when I was six. He loved her more than life and never got over losing her. He'd have done anything for her and for us. But I don't even know how to begin to process or understand it."

"Take all the time you need," Jay said. "I'm not going anywhere."

"Thank you."

Jay didn't speak for a long moment, but she could hear him moving across the floorboards to the other side of the loft. The old barn had been a fixture of her life for as long as she could remember, with its fading gray wood, which she presumed had once been brown, and its sloping roof, which had always seemed ready to drip shingles. She'd never understood why her father had wanted Jay to start repairing it when the house seemed like a much higher priority.

All her father would say was it had good bones.

A light switched on somewhere to her right. It was a gentle light, golden and soft. She opened her eyes slowly and looked around, thankful that time, the rain and her tears had lessened the pain in her eyes. Now she could make out the colorful weave of the thick rag rug beneath her and the pattern of the giant pillows leaning against the wall. There was also a single camp chair, a small folding metal table, a simple cot with nothing but a sleeping bag on it and an upside-down crate behind it holding a water bottle, notepad and Bible.

At the far end of the attic, she could barely make out some kind of huge pattern on the far brick wall made of lines, squares and rectangles. But the actual details of what she was looking at was still shrouded in darkness. Like the mystery surrounding her, she could only see a little, and the more she could see, the more questions it raised. She prayed for wisdom.

She heard a click. Through her blurry vision, she could see Jay crouching over a small cooler. He sloshed some liquid over a bandana and brought it to her. She reached for it and recognized it from the smell immediately.

"Milk, right?" she said. Her fingertips brushed his as she pulled it from his hand.

"Yup," he said.

"My dad always said dairy was best for burns," she said. "Specifically yogurt when you accidentally eat something spicy, like hot peppers, and milk for actual pepper spray. But I've never actually tried it. He was pretty daring in what he let us do but actually burning our senses was a step too far."

She pressed it against her eyes and immediately felt the cold soothing sensation easing her pain in a way the rain hadn't. She closed her eyes again and felt Jay sit down beside her.

"I never thought of my childhood as anything weird, different or out of the ordinary," she said. "What child does? For all I knew, everyone's father tucked them into a bed every night with a combination of survival skills, Bible verses and made-up fairy tales."

Dad had called the fairy-tale land Cymbafalls. The stories had been about four daring princesses, very obviously based on them, and the various innocents they rescued from a villain called the Shadow through a combination of compassion, skill and wit. She didn't know how he'd come up with them, but they'd made her feel invincible and like she could change the world. Maybe that's how she'd ended up working in a legal aid office and wanting to be a lawyer for those who couldn't afford one. She listened as Jay folded his long legs beneath him until he was sitting cross-legged. His knee bumped lightly against hers. It was comforting to feel him there.

"So, what did my dad tell you about my mom?" she asked.

"Walter told me that he'd had a best friend in high school who he was very close to," Jay started. "Best person he knew. Someone he would've done anything for."

"That would be my mom," she said. "There was nobody else who ever fit that bill for him." Unexpected and hot tears rose to her eyes. She pressed the milk-soaked rag against them. "I'm relieved actually, even though I don't understand, because at least that makes sense."

"He said that when they graduated high school, she had this dream of working in the big city," Jay went on. "He didn't think it was a good idea and they quarreled about it, but she was determined, so off she went."

She chuckled softly. Yeah, that sounded exactly like how her dad would tell the story.

"He didn't hear from her for almost two months, when she called in the middle of the night to say she was in trouble," Jay said. "She said that Franklin Vamana had taken a líking to her when he'd spotted her waiting tables in one of his nightclubs, started taking her out places and insisted she move into a condo in one of his buildings for a ridiculously good rent. It was like a fairy tale. But then she realized he had a temper and became suspicious of the fact people who Franklin railed against kept disappearing. Then one night she saw him backhand a busboy so hard he fell, hit his head and died. When she insisted they go to the police, Franklin said if she breathed a word to anyone, he'd kill her and her family. None of you would ever be safe from him."

Leia sucked in a painful breath.

"One of my dad's bedtime fairy-tale stories went like that," she said slowly. "A lot like that. Only in his version it was an evil villain who'd captured a brave queen. In his telling, a poor farmer helped her escape."

The farmer had been in love with her. He'd married the queen and they'd had the four princess daughters before she died.

"In this version, too," Jay said. "She called your dad at three in the morning from a pay phone and told him that she was terrified and couldn't escape because Franklin had taken her on this trip to Niagara Falls and now she was stranded at this hotel he'd booked with no way to get home. He'd even taken her purse. Your dad dropped everything and drove through the night to find her and bring her home."

"When was that?" she asked.

"August," he said.

"And my parents were married in September," she said, "and I was born almost ten months later." She blew out a hard breath. "Just like in the fairy tale."

"Your dad loved your mom," Jay said gently. "If he didn't tell anyone that she'd spent two months working for Franklin Vamana and witnessed him kill someone, he did it to keep you all safe."

"But why wasn't she braver?" Leia asked. She dropped the milk-soaked rag from her eyes and blinked up at Jay. "Why just change her name, make an anonymous call to police and hide evidence of a serial killer in the farmhouse?"

"I don't know," Jay admitted.

His face swam before hers now as her vision cleared and for a moment the depths of compassion filling his dark eyes was so strong and comforting that she had to grit her teeth to keep from tumbling into his arms and crying.

"Hey, your eyes are looking a lot better," he said. "A lot less puffy and red. By the look of things, Dunlop got you with a pretty brutal direct shot."

She felt her chin rise.

"Like I told you before, he didn't set the pepper spray off. I did—"

"Yeah, I know a couple of guys on the force who've accidentally taken a hit to the face—"

"It wasn't an accident!" Her voice sharpened defensively and she didn't quite know why. All she knew was that she was tired of feeling like a victim of circumstances, secrets and crimes. "I quite deliberately set the pepper spray off a few inches from my own face."

Jay's mouth opened but no words came out. She let the thought sink in for a moment and raised the cloth back to her eyes again.

"It was the smartest option I had to keep that monster from kidnapping me," she said. "He basically showed me that he had pepper spray and a gun, and said that one way or the other I was going with him. He didn't care if he subdued me or shot me, as long as I could still talk. I knew the rule of thumb for kidnappings was never let anyone take you to a secondary crime scene. And that pepper spray wasn't fatal. I had a much higher probability of surviving a car crash than a gunshot at close quarters."

Wow, she really did sound like her dad. She wondered if Jay could hear it, too.

"I tried to grab the wheel first," she went on, "before I saw he had a gun. I couldn't reach the gun, but that pepper spray was just inches from my face. So, I grabbed his hand with both of mine, closed my eyes, turned my head and deployed it."

Jay let out a low whistle.

"If something bad was going to happen to me, it was going to happen on my own terms," she added. Jay didn't respond. "You think I'm an idiot, don't you?"

"No," he said. "I'm impressed. Incredibly so. It was risky but smart. You're one of the bravest people I've ever met."

Unexpected heat rose to her face that had nothing to do with the pepper spray. The back of his hand brushed against her knee. Instinctively she stretched her free hand toward it and her fingers touched his hand.

"Oh," she said, finding her mouth struggling to form words. "I learned it all from my dad."

"He told you things," Jay said. "You're the one who remembered them and figured out how to put them into action."

"Thank you," she said, not knowing what else to say.

He turned his hand into hers and their fingertips linked. For a moment neither of them said anything. They just sat there, their hands lightly touching, and listened to the sound of the storm pound around them.

"Now what?" she asked.

"Now we regroup and then figure out a new way to contact my colleagues in law enforcement, warn your sister Sally not to come home tomorrow morning and escape from here," Jay said. "And I'd rather wait a few minutes for you to recover than try to run around doing this without you. I kept you in the dark for far too long."

So had her father by the sound of it.

"I wish we'd talked about all this a lot sooner," Jay added after a long moment. "I know I did the right thing in not breaking my cover. But your father had specifically made you and your sisters not knowing a condition of his cooperation. Still, I wish I'd told you."

"I wish my father had told me," she said. "So what if he and my mom broke up for a while and she moved to the city before they were married?"

"He thought he was protecting you," Jay said.

"By not telling us that our mom had witnessed a murder and had evidence of a serial killer?" she asked. Then she sat up sharply, pulled her hand away from Jay and opened her eyes. "Wait, why do these criminals think my mother is still alive if she died of cancer when I was six? Why don't they know her married name?"

Jay ran his hand over the back of his head. She leaned back and looked where the rain beat against the skylight, running down the glass in near invisible silver tracks. When

Jay had blocked up the windows at either end of the barn's loft last summer and instead put in skylights that pointed directly to the clouds above, she'd thought it was for insulation purposes. Now she realized it also meant someone in the loft could have a light on without anyone on the ground noticing.

What else hadn't she noticed? For all the times she'd met Jay and they'd talked in the barn below them, how had she never realized the hideout he was constructing just above her head?

"My guess is that Franklin Vamana has not been tracking your family," he said, "and that something suddenly made him remember your mother. Maybe it's the fact he's been reportedly having health problems recently, but I think it's more likely that the discovery of the two John Does encased in cement made him realize his past crimes could be coming back to haunt him and he needed to tie up loose ends. It's possible he somehow found out about the anonymous call she made to the police thirty-five years ago."

"But how did his goons track her here?" she asked.

"Maybe he knew she loved your father and so tracked down his family home," Jay suggested. "If Dunlop was trying to build a relationship with your dad last year, the timeline would fit."

"Is it possible someone found out my dad was working with you?" she asked.

"I really hope not," Jay said. "Maintaining cover is everything to me. It really meant a lot to me that you didn't tell Dunlop. Thanks for that."

"No problem," she said. "I did call you Jay the farmhand, though, and said I wasn't leaving without you."

"That should be fine," he said.

"Why is it so important to you that you stay undercover?" she asked.

"Because this isn't just one assignment for me," he said. "This is what I want to do for the rest of my life. A few months ago, a legend in the Royal Canadian Mounted Police retired. His name was Liam Bearsmith and he worked with my mentor, Detective Jessica Stone. Bearsmith spent over two decades in undercover police work, taking down countless bad guys without his cover ever being blown. He's a legend. And I want to do something like that with my life, too."

"What happened to him?" Leia asked. "Was he killed?"

"No," Jay said softly. "He fell in love."

She turned to look at him again for a long moment. His dark-eyed gaze met hers. The lines of his handsome face and strong form were half-hidden in lights and shadows. She could feel his breath against her face. The familiar woodsy rugged smell of his T-shirt filled her senses, tugging on memories of embraces she'd tried so hard to forget.

She bit her lip. "What happens if you fall in love?"

"I guess I'm going to have to push those feelings away," he said, his voice dropping to a whisper, "and keep them from interfering in my life."

He said the words like it was possible to switch off one's heart like a faucet. Did he really feel that way? Was he really so heartless?

And yet all she'd have to do was move a couple inches and she'd be nestled up against his strong chest the way she had countless times before. And if he'd tilted his head just a little, his lips would've brushed hers in a kiss.

Instead, he leaped to his feet, like a cat did when the clouds above suddenly stopped blocking the hot sun from its fur.

Suddenly she was thankful she hadn't let herself kiss him. He'd broken her heart before, she reminded herself, and he'd disappear from her life again. He'd told her as much. She had to keep him out of her heart, just as it seemed he was determined to do with her.

"Can I show you something?" he asked. "If your eyes are up to it. I find it helps if I map everything out visually, so I can look at it all."

"Sure," she said, "my sister Sally is the same."

He hesitated and then reached out his hand as if offering to help her up. She didn't take it and pulled herself to her feet without it.

"Okay if I turn on another light?" he asked.

"Yeah," she said. "My eyes just feel like bad hay fever now. The milk definitely helped."

He reached underneath the cot and pulled out a long thin light that almost reminded her of the kind crime scene investigators used. He walked to the far end of the loft, clipped it on an unseen hook and switched it on.

Golden light washed down the wall like a waterfall. She gasped. It was covered in photographs, both large and small, along with newspaper clippings, sticky notes, words scribbled between them in chalk and long lines linking them. She stepped back, her brain swimming to take it all in. There were photographs clumped together under headings like Victims?, Accomplices? and Vamana Enterprises. In one corner were photos of her and her family.

"This is what I couldn't risk anyone seeing last summer," he said. "Of course, I took it down when I moved out and reassembled it on my apartment wall when I got home. I was actually rebuilding it here tonight when I heard your car pull up."

He turned to face her.

"Do you get it now?" he asked. "This is why I had to create a hideaway in the barn. I needed a place to work on the case and put all the pieces together. And I couldn't risk anyone seeing it."

This is what he'd been secretly working on every time she snuck away to the barn to meet him? Every time he'd held her, kissed her or they'd sat on the hay bales discussing their hopes and dreams for the future, this had been hiding away in the barn, just feet above her head? How foolish she must have looked when she called the barn their special place or assumed he spent so much time there because of her.

"What are you thinking?" he asked. "You look like you've seen a ghost."

She turned away. "I… I don't know what to say."

Lord, I feel so foolish right now. There are much more important things than my own broken heart, and I know that. But right now I can't see past how I feel.

"Please," he said. His voice wavered uncertainly. "Just talk to me. I've never shown my process to anyone like this. I want to know what you're thinking."

"No," she said. "You really don't." And she didn't want to say it.

"Please, Leia." Jay stepped closer to her. "Just say it. Whatever it is, I can take it."

She looked up into his face.

"Did you kiss me that first time to keep me from seeing all this?" she asked. "Considering how easy you seem to find it to switch off your emotions, was our relationship just a big fake lie to maintain your cover?"

He took a step back and sucked in a breath. His chest ached as if her words had hit him like a literal punch to the gut. Did she really think he'd held her in his arms, stroked her hair and told her things that he'd never told another person, just to keep her from blowing his cover?

Was that what she thought of him?

He turned and walked a few steps back toward the other end of the barn's loft, hoping she wouldn't see the visceral pain in his eyes. Leia really did have absolutely no idea what she'd meant to him or how much he'd cared about her.

And she'd never know how close he'd come to giving up his career for her.

He closed his eyes and prayed for God's guidance.

In an instant, a memory swept over his mind. He remembered standing with her in the barn, cupping her face in his hands as the rain pounded down outside. He'd been just a breath away from kissing her lips, with their eyes locked on each other's faces and the sound of their breaths mingling with the sound of the summer storm, when he'd realized he was about to ask her to marry him.

That was the moment he'd known that he'd crossed a line inside his own heart that he'd never imagined he could and never would again. With every foolish beat, it was crying out that he'd never feel this way about anyone else ever again, and that he'd never forgive himself if he let her go. Meanwhile his head had been yelling that he really needed to be sure what he was doing.

So, he'd tore himself away from her and driven the hour to Kilpatrick, where he'd sat down with his mentor, Jess, who specialized in investigating special crimes, and her new husband, Travis, who'd recently given up a career in law enforcement for civilian work that enabled him to raise their two adopted children. There in their living room surrounded by children's toys and drawings reminding him of the kind of life he'd chosen not to have, they'd gently but firmly told him the truth he needed to hear.

Yes, he'd face disciplinary action if his relationship with Leia came to light and be taken off the Phantom Killer case. And yes, being married and having a family might limit the kind of undercover work he could take. But that he needed to follow his heart and his God.

They'd also told him, kindly, that there was no guarantee that if he gave up his career for her that she'd love and want him back once she knew the truth. And that had been the moment he'd realized he couldn't risk his future on a woman who might never love him back after he'd kept the truth from her. He told them he was going to call things off with Leia immediately, before it went too far, because no matter how he might feel about her she had no idea who he really was.

Then he'd focused on not letting himself feel what was going on in his own heart, just like he had after his father had died. And that had been that.

"No," he said stiffly. "It wasn't some kind of ploy or game. I genuinely liked you." *So much more than liked you.* "It was an unfortunate and foolish breach of protocol, and once a mentor reminded me what was at risk, I knew it had to end. I'm sorry. More than you know. But it wasn't a lie or part of my cover. It was a mistake."

Thunder crashed outside, drowning out his words before he could say anything more. There were so many things he wanted to tell her and so much he wanted her to know.

"Okay," Leia said. "That's all I was wondering. Now, how about you explain this board to me and tell me what I'm looking at. I have no clue what time it is, but I'm guessing we're down to four hours before Sally gets here. And I don't know about you, but I'm ready to get out of here."

Right. He blew out a long breath and placed a hand over the back of his neck. Then he turned to look at the board, being just as careful not to meet her eyes as she seemed to be not wanting to meet his.

"The Phantom Killer, if real, is one of Canada's more prolific serial killers," he said. "But until recently, no bodies were ever found. So, police have been very reluctant to classify anyone as dead, let alone murdered. Also, all the disappearances took place over a three-year period, some thirty-five years ago. Now, it's not unheard of for serial killers to stop murdering people for a while and go underground. Sometimes they have a change of life circumstances, find another way to impose control on people that they find more fulfilling, or get spooked. But it makes it harder to find them."

"What kind of evidence could you even find after all this time?" she asked. "Even when you find the bodies, I imagine anything they were buried with will be completely decomposed."

"A lot of serial killers keep mementos or souvenirs of their victims," he said. "In fact, the two corpses we've found so far each had a bone missing. It's possible the killer saved them." The thought was so distasteful he winced like there was something bitter on his tongue. "If police can get enough evidence to search Franklin Vamana's home, we might be able to find evidence he killed these people."

Was that what Leia's mother had stolen? Were a serial killers mementos hidden somewhere in the farmhouse?

Leia frowned as if the same unpleasant thought had crossed her mind, too.

"But this group here are known criminals," she said, pointing to the cluster of photos labeled Associates. "Because that's Dunlop right there, that's Stan, there's Ross and I'm pretty sure I saw that big guy there around here, too." She pointed to a bearded man who looked almost sixty. "Willie Hirsch. I think he's the one I called Stompy Boots."

"Yeah, I think I saw him, too." Jay wasn't sure what to make of how quickly she'd changed gears. "That's four out of five. The only one I don't see is Ben, the guy I jumped outside my garage. But if I'm right, he's very new to crime and was roped in to be the patsy if things go wrong or someone needs to take the fall. You want to know the scary thing? I've had these faces on my board for months before tonight. I literally made it my life's goal to take some of these guys down. And I had no idea they were actually working for Franklin or that they'd come after you. This bunch here are all known criminals who've had some association with Vamana Enterprises in the past. Maybe they accepted a bribe or worked for either Franklin or his sister in some capacity."

Her eyes rose to twin glossy photos of Franklin and his older sister, Esther. Both were in their late sixties, but looked younger with tanned skin, blue eyes, toothy smiles and silver hair.

"Esther runs Indigo Iris, the cosmetics company based in Niagara," Leia said. "I never really wore makeup until I started working to pay for law school. But I remember being really excited when I heard of the company, thinking she might have purple eyes like me. I was really disappointed when I found out she didn't."

"Apparently her mother did," Jay said. "Rumor is that Franklin cut Esther out of their inheritance when their parents died. Now that Franklin is sick, Esther is trying to use that as leverage to get a piece of his company."

"Nice family," Leia said, and rolled her eyes.

"I don't know the details of Franklin's illness," he said. "But it might explain why he stopped killing, or at the very least why he'd be sending proxies like these men instead of doing the dirty work himself."

"Got it," she said. She nodded slowly as if taking in the Vamana siblings and their criminal associates, then she turned her back on them and toward the victims. "Tell me about them."

He took a deep breath and felt a fresh confidence come over them.

"This is Alicia," he said, pointing to a smiling woman with frizzy hair. "She was nineteen, a waitress and single mom of a little boy named Daniel. This is Tobias, aged sixty-two. He was living on the streets but had served his country for two tours in the military before falling on hard times."

His hand flitted from face to face, introducing each missing person like an old friend. Jonathan, who was a busboy and who they now assumed Leia's mother had seen murdered. He had a criminal record for petty theft. Nathaniel worked as a cook at the homeless shelter where he lived, and Calvin sold drugs on the street corner. Elec-

tra and Marissa were both struggling danc-
ers in their twenties who also waited tables.
Janet was raising her four grandkids while
running a kiosk cart selling plastic trinkets
to tourists.

"Each dot on this map," he said, pointing,
"indicates a place where one of the victims
was last seen. As you'll see they're all south
of Bloor, east of Yonge and west of Bayview.
That whole area just north of Lake Ontario
is home to several Vamana Enterprise properties. I know there's no obvious surface
pattern to the victims at first, as they're all
different ages, body types and ethnic back-
grounds. But they were all living close to
the poverty line and struggling to make it
economically. It made them vulnerable. It
meant police were more likely to overlook
or excuse away their disappearances."

Had the Phantom Killer stolen something from each of them to commemorate
his crime? If so, did he now have that evidence stashed away somewhere?

"The least of these," she murmured. She
turned to Jay. A warm light shone in her violet eyes. "That's what my dad would call
them. He always reminded us of what Jesus
said in the Book of Matthew that how we
treat the poor, the hungry, the imprisoned

and those in need was a reflection of how we treated Him. Dad worked that message into a lot of his fairy tales actually. I… I can see why this case mattered so much to him. I don't get why he hid it from us, but I get why he contacted you. He'd never be able to get over knowing someone had gotten away on preying on people like this."

Something warmed in his heart. Yes! That's exactly how he felt, too. If only she knew just how long he'd wanted to share this with her.

"If we're right about your mother being his secret friend, she couldn't, either," Jay said. "She made him promise on her deathbed that when God told him the timing was right he'd do whatever he could to ensure Franklin got justice."

"She made him promise to protect my sisters and me, too," Leia said. Then her gaze flitted to the solitary picture of a man in his late-thirties with round glasses, a trim beard and a goofy smile. Her eyes widened. "That's Jayce Starling, the journalist."

"You know him?" Jay asked.

"Yeah," she said. "My dad was a huge fan of his books of essays on homelessness, affordable housing and veterans. I've read them all more than once."

"He was my dad," Jay said. His voice caught in his throat as a wave of unwanted emotions surged in his chest. "I was named Jayce after him. With the *CE*. It's an old family name he wanted passed down. My mom called me Jay. My middle name was Brock. I changed it when I left home."

Her eyes widened. "I had no idea."

Jay found himself choosing his words carefully. "Did you know he was an alcoholic?"

"I did." She nodded. "He wrote a lot about how struggling with his own addiction brought him closer to God and opened his hearts to the needs of others."

"He walked out the door when I was four and never came back," Jay said. "Police were convinced he'd just relapsed, walked out on his family and left my mom for another woman. The newspaper ran stories with headlines like Alcoholic Writer Vanishes. But my mom was convinced that he loved us and the Phantom Killer took him out because he was researching the missing people of Toronto who nobody else cared about."

"Do you think that Franklin Vamana killed your father?" she asked.

"Police don't," he said. "It was so thoroughly debunked as just some wishful thinking on my mom's part that it wasn't considered a serious reason for me not to take this case. I was even given permission to use his old notes on the victims to build a profile for my case."

"But what do you think?" she asked.

Her hand brushed his and he found himself taking it. He thought he was standing beside the most incredible and beautiful person in the entire world and that anyone in their right mind would've been running from him right now instead of holding his hand.

"I don't know what to think," he admitted.

"Neither do I," she said. "But I know that I'm done hiding, and that you and I are going to take this killer down, starting now."

SIX

She fought the urge to pace, but just ended up bouncing on the balls of her feet, as if the kinetic energy of her body moving was the only thing keeping her from falling apart. She'd just told Jay that they were going to step up, do something, escape the farm and get justice for the victims of the Phantom Killer. The drumbeat of motivation in her heart as she scanned the faces of the victims felt so strong it was like she could charge out into the fray and take down a sea of enemies. If only she could figure out how.

She glanced at Jay. His eyes were closed, and his lips were moving silently, and she realized he was probably praying. She and Jay had prayed together many times last summer. Their shared faith had been something they'd embraced. And now, even as she was getting to know him again and learning who he really was, it made her happy to realize his faith had been real, and not part of his cover. His belief in caring for those in need was even deeper than she realized. No wonder he'd seemed so happy when she told him she was working at a legal aid office and dreamed of becoming a lawyer for those in need who couldn't afford one.

It was ironic. She'd worried about what her father would think if he found out she had feelings for Jay, and yet he'd been the one man that Dad had decided to trust with his deepest secrets. She'd always feared that when she caught a glimpse of the man behind the mask Jay wore, it would shatter her image of him. Now that she was actually getting to see who the man behind the cover really was, she liked him even more than before.

It was ironic, considering she now knew that very pursuit of justice that she admired was what would keep them from ever being together in the way she once hoped they could be.

Okay, Leia, focus. It was a simple problem. They were trapped at her farm, in the middle of nowhere, with no way to contact the outside world. She'd spent her entire life growing up at this farm and knew its ins and outs better than anyone, even if Jay had built a secret hideaway in the barn without her knowledge.

Lord, help me think outside the box.

An idea struck. She turned to Jay.

"Your team is tech-savvy, right?" she asked.

"Jess's husband, Travis, has state-of-the-art computer skills," he said. "Plus, she has a tech consultant named Seth, who claims to be one of the best computer hackers in the world."

"Okay, well, you'll remember we have an old computer in the basement?" she asked. The basement was only partially finished, with old plank staircases and drop-ceiling tiles. "It's a big giant brick of a thing that takes an hour to do anything and can barely even run the internet. My dad basically gave it to my sisters and me to play around with when we were kids and he upgraded to a better one."

"Yeah," he said. "Didn't see anything much of value on it when it came to the case, but I made an external backup of it, anyway."

An uncomfortable feeling pricked at the back of her neck.

"You went through and copied my childhood computer?" she asked. "I wrote all my school essays on that thing. I wrote letters to my high school crushes, and poems. I even had my diary on it!"

He opened his mouth, then closed it again, and she watched as his jaw moved, as if rolling various words around on his tongue to see how they tasted.

"Yes," he said finally. "I did and I'm sorry. I can imagine I'd feel really lousy if I was in your shoes. But I didn't read any of it. I simply copied the data and ran it through an algorithm for anything possibly related to my case. The only thing I actually remember were pictures your sister Sally drew of maps from stories in your father's fairy-tale world. There were these rainbows, rivers, islands, trees and twin waterfalls. They were incredible."

"Cymbafalls," she said. "That's the name my father gave his imaginary world. Sadly, he forgot the stories as he grew older and we never wrote them down, so they're lost forever. But they're oddly similar to what you were telling me about the Phantom Killer's alleged victims. In each one, the princesses teamed up to rescue a different person who'd been captured by the Shadow…"

Her voice trailed off almost as if a thought had flitted past her mind too quickly for her to grasp. She'd never questioned the fact her father made up stories to tell at bedtime. Could he have based them on real events?

"I think we might be able to use the computer to contact the outside world," she said. "We used to have an old phone line to the house that was really degraded and kept cutting out. When my dad had the new phone line installed, they never took out the old wiring. So, my sisters and I attached this really ancient modem to it that my dad didn't use anymore and we discovered that as long as we sent very basic and quick, text-based emails with nothing attached, they'd get through about fifty percent of the time. It's possible that when they cut the main phone line they didn't get that one."

"And if not, we have a fifty-fifty possibility of getting a message out," he said.

"Yup," she said, "and we'll have to use my old email address because that's the only email program loaded on the machine."

"Well, it's something," Jay said, "and something is better than nothing. So, we sneak back into the criminal-filled house, make our way to the basement, fire up an old modem and hope that everyone checks their spam filters."

"That's why I asked if your team was

tech-savvy," she said. "If so, hopefully the fact it's an old messaging system won't throw them."

"Knowing my contacts, it might intrigue them," Jay said.

He rubbed his hands together, then reached for a roll of paper sitting on the floor, took it over to the metal folding table and spread it out. It was a blueprint of the farmhouse.

"The way I see it," he said, "is we move along the tree line until we reach the back of the house. Then we create a diversion, cut through the kitchen, head down the back staircase, through the family room and we're there. It'll be very risky, but it's our best option."

She almost chuckled.

"Or," she said, "we simply cut through this much shorter path to this side of the house and climb straight down into the basement."

"That won't work," Jay said, but doubt hovered in his eyes. "I thought your dad installed locks on all the basement windows."

"He did," she said. "But stop thinking like a cop and start thinking like one of four incredibly strong-willed and adventurous girls who grew up on a farm in the middle of nowhere. He installed everything when we were tiny, and if he didn't notice something was loose or broken we didn't always tell him. Specifically, there's a vent right here between the two windows that's loose. Quinn used to use it to sneak in the house at night."

His eyebrow quirked. "I thought you said she snuck out using the rope ladder."

"She did," Leia said. "But Rose always pulled it back up when she left. And if Rose was asleep when Quinn came back and didn't lower the ladder back down, she'd sneak in this way."

Jay snorted a laugh.

"Hey, Quinn's now one of the top outdoor exploration and climbing guides in Canada," Leia said. "She literally guides people up glaciers. Thankfully, we know it's still possible to slip in and out through it, because Sally figured out that's how Moses was getting in."

"And remind me who Moses is?" Jay asked.

"A small brown, white and black tabby cat who sometimes shows up and pretends he lives here," Leia said. "We're not sure where he's coming from and he never stays long. He's very independent. But he loves hiding in bags and more than once Sally has opened her diaper bag or suitcase and been startled to find the little cat hidden inside. Sally always leaves a saucer and some treats out for him in the kitchen. I'm sure she'd appreciate it if we managed to find him and rescue him, too. But he might not be here. I haven't seen him all night."

Jay paused and his eyes searched his meticulously detailed wall of information for a moment.

"Well," he said finally. "I've got to admit, I wish I'd come to stay at this farm and get to know your entire family sometime when there wasn't crime involved."

"Maybe when this is all over, I'll invite you over for a family dinner," she said.

He smiled and she felt warmth spread to her cheeks. Then just as quickly the grin faded.

Guess undercover detectives didn't do friendships, either.

He dropped through the hatch first, back into the lower part of the barn and disappeared from view once he'd looked around. Then his face reappeared in the opening. He looked up at her.

"Come on," he said. "I'll catch you. There is a rope ladder, but I'd need to hook it up."

She swung her legs through the opening, slid her body off the ledge and tumbled down into his arms without even pausing to question it. He caught her to his chest and held her there for an instant as the smell of the hay, the old barn and the wet earth outside surrounded them on all sides.

They were mere steps away from the place where they'd first kissed. And maybe it was the familiarity of the place or the closeness of the conversation they'd shared, but in that moment everything inside her wanted to just let her head fall into the crook of his neck and savor the feeling of his arms around her. She wanted to wrap her arms around him in a hug, kiss his lips and tell him she'd missed him and forgave him.

Instead, she eased herself out of his arms as he set her down on the floor and stepped back.

Jay wasn't asking her forgiveness, let alone asking her to kiss him or go back to the kind of relationship they'd had before. He wasn't even implying he wanted to be friends. They'd been thrown together by circumstances, nothing more. And once they got help and made their way to safety, who was to say he wouldn't just disappear out of her life and she'd never see him again?

Jay squeezed her hand for a brief moment and prayed aloud, asking God to guide them. Then they made their way out of the barn and through the darkness, down a narrow path shrouded by old farm equipment and overgrown hedges. Rain lashed against them. The farmhouse loomed ahead in the storm. They crouched low beside the edge of the garage and paused. A figure was walking back and forth between the farmhouse and garage, swinging his flashlight as he went like a sentry in the storm.

"I'm guessing that's Ben," Jay said. "I didn't want to risk killing him and couldn't arrest him, so I left him somewhere people could find him."

"So much for hoping they'd either found whatever they were after or given up and left," Leia whispered.

"I still wish I knew where they hid their vehicles and how they got here," Jay said. "There's something about this whole situation that still doesn't make sense. But right now, all I can afford to worry about is getting inside that building."

She held her breath as Jay's keen eyes tracked the man's motions. Jay counted slowly beneath his breath.

"His timing isn't very consistent," he said.

"But I think I've figured out when our best window is to make a run for it."

He reached down, took her hand and held it. They waited as the man with the flashlight strode past their hiding place, swinging the light in front of him like a minesweeper. Jay waited until he'd reached the edge of the driveway.

"Now," he whispered.

She clenched his hand. He leaped up and sprung, holding her hand tightly as they ran across the open ground in the darkness toward the side of the house. Her foot slipped and she tumbled to one knee on the wet grass, before Jay pulled her back up and they kept sprinting. The man with the flashlight turned back.

"Hey!" Ben shouted. The flashlight's beam swung wide, bouncing its light between the barn and farmhouse. "Hey, is somebody there?"

Jay and Leia reached the farmhouse and their hands slipped from each other's grasp as they dove for the relative safety of the side of the wall. She lay flat on her stomach on the ground and pressed herself against the wall. Then she started to crawl slowly toward the vent, hearing the faint shuffle of Jay behind her.

The man with the flashlight shouted for backup. Within moments, Willie had charged around the side of the building, adding a second swinging beam of light to the darkness. "What's going on?"

"I think I heard something!" Ben said.

"Is it her?"

"I don't know! Just help me look!"

She reached the vent, slid her fingers under the edge of the metal and pulled. Her fingers slipped, refusing to find a grip. She clenched her jaw and prayed. But still it wouldn't budge. The criminals were still shouting and swearing. She couldn't see or hear Jay anywhere. She swung her body around in the darkness, braced her foot against the vent and kicked. It swung free.

Thank You, God!

She slid her feet into the open space and pushed herself through. Her body slithered through the vent and landed back in the small basement office.

"Jay!" she whispered. "I'm in. Come on."

There was no answer. Nothing but the sound of the pouring rain and shouting voices filtered through the vent. Fear seized her heart.

Where was Jay?

The movement in the darkness was so

swift she barely managed to clamp her hand over her mouth to keep from screaming as she felt something soft bounce onto her shoulder from a pile of boxes before leaping up and disappearing in a brown and white streak through the vent.

It was Moses the cat.

She willed her beating heart to calm.

"Jay?" she tried again. "Where are you?"

Lord, please may he be all right.

Then she heard the sound of a gunshot split the air.

Jay froze, lying outside on the ground, with his body pressed against the damp earth and a single bright beam of light stretching across the ground directly between him and the hole in the wall through which Leia had just disappeared. He felt a cat skim past his body, scampering over his back before leaping down and brushing against his legs. Then it disappeared into the darkness.

Jay held his breath and prayed for help. He couldn't risk moving until the man who'd dropped the flashlight picked it up again. Otherwise, he'd crawl right through the beam of light. But if the man swung the light in his direction when he grabbed it, his next bullet could have Jay's name on it.

"Hold your fire!" Ben shouted, his words laced with profanities.

"I saw someone!" Willie snapped and swore.

"It was a cat!" Ben said. "You shot at a cat and almost hit it!"

"It was a man!"

"Then where is he?"

Jay lay as still as he could and kept his body tucked against the wall, waiting for the flashlight beam to move.

"We're not supposed to kill her," Ben shouted.

A chill ran down Jay's spine. Yeah, Ben had said that before, but it hadn't really hit Jay until now. By "she" did they mean Leia's mother? Or Leia herself? And why did Franklin need either of them alive?

"I told you, it was a man!" Willie roared like he was moments away from physically punching the younger man. "You don't get a say in what happens to who here. Your job is to be quiet and tell us if you see anyone."

He snatched up his flashlight. Its beam bounced across the wall inches in front of Jay.

"You shot at a cat!"

The bickering voices began to fade as the two criminals walked down toward the front of the house. And even though Jay knew he'd left Leia alone in the basement, part of him fought the urge to follow. He needed to hear more.

Instead, he crawled as fast as he could to the hole in the wall through which Leia had disappeared and as he drew closer he could hear her whispering his name.

He slid his body beside it and looked in. There was Leia, faintly lit by an unseen light source, fear and worry filling her eyes.

She slid her hands over her lips as if to stop herself from crying out. "Jay!"

"Yeah, it's me."

"You okay?" she asked. "I heard a gunshot."

"Yeah, they tried to hit the cat and missed," he said. "Give me a second."

She stepped back and disappeared from view. He pivoted and slid his body through the hole feetfirst. It was such a tight squeeze that for a moment his shoulders stuck, leaving his body in the basement and his face still outside in the rain, until he wriggled himself through.

He landed crouched on the balls of his feet in the cold and dark basement. As he stood, he felt Leia rush into his arms and envelop him in a hug. Instinctively he felt his arms part as he hugged her back.

"You okay?" he asked.

"I was worried," she said. "You disappeared and I thought I was going to have to do this alone."

He pulled her tighter to his chest, feeling as if, just for a moment, that broken part of him had fit back into place. His hand stroked along the back of her head and tangled through her hair.

"You can't get rid of me that easily," he said. "I promise. Until this is over you won't ever have to do it alone."

She didn't answer but she didn't pull away, either. Neither did he. He just let the hug linger for one long moment.

Lord, why does it feel like my feelings for this woman are at risk of coming back now? I tried so hard to move past them and put them behind me. It had been hard enough to try and get over her when they were apart. When he'd seen her at her father's graveside from a distance, it had taken all the strength he had to keep from running to her side, pulling her into his arms and comforting her. And now, just a few hours back in her company, he remembered how much he'd admired her, cared about her and wished they could build a life together. *How can my heart still be so weak? Help me be strong.*

It was Leia who pulled away from the embrace and stepped back. That's when he saw where the light was coming from. A heavy, plastic yellow flashlight sat facedown on the carpeted floor, casting just the smallest pool of light there. It was the kind he'd had as a kid that gobbled up large batteries for not much light in return. He walked to the window, felt for the vent grate and pulled it back over the hole, blocking out the rain and hopefully keeping anyone outside from seeing the light.

Leia picked the flashlight up and swung it around the room. The office seemed even smaller than he remembered and packed on all sides with old-fashioned metal filing cabinets and Bankers boxes, all of whose contents he'd once unsuccessfully poured through and which now lay tossed in a deluge of white paper on the floor. A door to one side led through to the family room, and an unfinished staircase led up to the main floor. The computer's large and sturdy bulk took up most of the small desk.

"Have you managed to get it running?" he asked.

"Not yet," she said. "I was waiting for you before I started moving things around. Glad you made it."

"Yeah, I am, too," he said, despite the fact he wished he'd been able to hear more of the criminals' conversation.

"What's wrong?" Leia asked. "You're frowning."

Was he that obvious around her? How had he ever managed to keep his true identity from her for so long? Or had she somehow, despite it all, managed to see the real him back then even through the mask?

"I was just thinking that something about this whole case doesn't make sense," he admitted.

"A lot of it doesn't make sense," she said. "What specifically?" She pressed the computer's large gray button twice and when nothing happened pushed some boxes aside and slid around behind the desk and fiddled with the cords. "One second, the power bar needs to be reset."

The computer sprung to life with a loud chime as the decades-old operating system began to load. He lunged for the computer and slapped his hands over the speakers to block out the noise. Leia did so, too, and for a moment their hands overlapped as they tried to block the sound. Then the noise stopped, and a static blue screen appeared with a colored flag. White text assured them that despite appearances it was loading.

Leia blew out a long breath and dropped into the chair.

"So far so good," she said. "Now we wait to see if it actually works. So, why were you frowning?"

"I'm not even sure how to put it into words," he admitted.

"Try," she said. "Pretend I'm a fellow officer or your mentor, someone who you respect who isn't connected to the case."

"You *are* someone I respect, a whole lot," he said. He sat on the staircase and stared at the unmoving screen. "How many criminals did Vamana send here tonight?"

"Five," she said, like the answer was obvious, "as far as we know. Stan, Ross and Willie kidnapped me when I walked through the door. Ben was patrolling outside the house at the same time, and Dunlop kidnapped me and was killed by Stan. Why?"

The blue loading screen disappeared, followed by a brief black screen and then the desktop. An hourglass spun. Leia moved the mouse over to an icon on the bottom of the screen, but nothing happened when she clicked.

"That's a whole lot of men for an assignment like this," Jay said. "Sending five people up to a barn in the middle of nowhere to steal some files and kidnap someone. And remember I recognized a handful of these from my research, so I know their services don't go cheap."

The computer grumbled mechanically as it slowly got around to opening programs.

"I forgot both how loud and how slow these machines used to be," Leia said. "For argument's sake, Franklin Vamana is very wealthy, and being accused of being a serial killer is a pretty serious crime. Why not send all the guys you've got?"

"Because why go to all this trouble and expense?" Jay countered. "If his only goal is to destroy all evidence that he's a serial killer, why not just burn down the farm killing everyone inside? Why search the house? Why try to take your late mother alive? It's almost like Franklin has another goal other than just getting rid of anything and anyone who could prove he's a killer."

"I don't know," Leia said. She turned back to the screen, sending dark hair cascading over her shoulder. She clicked an icon at the bottom of the screen again and this time it loaded. "I'm going to write the emails and hit Send before I turn the modem on. That way we're not setting off a loud modem before we're ready."

The email program opened, and she created a new message.

"I'm sending it to Sally, Quinn and Rose at once." She said the words out loud to him as she typed them. "'Urgent. It's Leia. I'm safe and hiding at the farm with Jay. Criminals have broken in and have already killed one of their own. Apparently, Dad was assisting in a cold case before he died. Call the police. Warn each other. Don't let Sally drive up. See you soon. I love you. Psalm 61:2b.'"

"'When my heart is overwhelmed, lead me to the rock that is higher than I,'" Jay quoted. "Why end with that verse?"

She felt herself blink.

"Dad used to quote it to us at bedtime," she said. "I knew if I used it my sisters would know the email really did come from me."

She got up from her chair and let him take over the computer. He didn't read what he wrote out loud and she didn't ask.

"All right, I'm done," he said. "I'm sending this to Jess and Travis in Kilpatrick, their tech guru and my supervisor. Hopefully one of them will get the message, they'll send rescue, the bad guys will be arrested and this will finally be over. You ready?"

"I'm ready," she said. She leaned over the desk and switched the modem on. "I hope this works."

The deafening screech of the modem springing to life filled the room.

A shout came from the floor above them. Then came the sound of footsteps pounding toward them.

Leia's face paled. "They've found us."

SEVEN

"Get behind me!" Jay yelled as he leaped in front of her, and then it was like everything was happening at once.

The modem screeched like an ancient machine trying to come to life. The icon on the screen spun futilely. She felt Jay's arm around her shoulders and his other on her waist as he half guided and half pulled her down to the floor. He rolled with her underneath the stairs and sheltered her with his body, and for a moment she didn't understand why.

Then gunfire filled the air above her. As she watched, the computer was riddled with bullets, shattering the screen, blowing holes in the case and sending broken fragments flying around the room. She clasped her hand over her mouth to keep from making a sound. She was helpless to do anything but watch until the machine was completely destroyed and the wall behind it was full of bullet holes.

Help us, Lord.

She had no idea if the messages for help were even sent and now her best hope to reach the outside world had been demolished into a mass of broken plastic and glass. The sound of gunfire stopped. Footsteps creaked on the steps as if someone was slowly walking down. It was Ross. Jay pulled away from her and leaped, snatching up the flashlight and wielding it like a baseball bat. His blow caught the man across the jaw. He grunted and fell back.

Jay tucked the flashlight into his belt and reached for Leia's hand. "Come on."

She leaped to her feet and followed as they pushed through the door into the huge basement rec room where she'd spent endless hours watching television, making crafts and building forts with her sisters. They pushed through another door and ran up the back staircase toward the main floor. They reached the landing outside the kitchen and listened. Silence fell from the other side of the door.

"I don't know if the emails went," she said.

"We can only hope," Jay said. "Now, if the

coast is clear we sprint straight through the back door and into the woods. Then when we're sure we're not being followed, we make it back to the loft in the barn and regroup."

"Okay," she said, and nodded. "If you've got your gun, why didn't you shoot him?"

"Because for now he thinks I'm a hapless farmhand who got caught up in all this," he said. "Once I pull my weapon, I run the risk of someone realizing I'm a cop. And if I kill him to keep from blowing my cover, when does it stop?" His hand caressed the side of her face. "But don't worry. I promise you that when it comes time to fire and I know it's my only option, I won't hesitate."

He eased the door open and they looked out.

Stan sat in the kitchen of her childhood home with his muddy boots up on the table. In one hand he swigged a drink from the handmade mug her little sister Rose had made and painted for their dad in elementary school. A sudden flash of visceral rage rose up inside her like a phoenix. Nobody touched Dad's favorite mug or put their filthy boots on her family's table. No one came into her home and destroyed it.

Stan turned, his feet smacking the floor as he reached for his gun.

But his hand never reached it. Because before he got the opportunity, Leia struck, yanking a heavy saucepan from the shelf just inside the door and hurling it at his head. A frying pan and soup pot followed, leaving the criminal helpless to do anything but try to dodge the projectiles. Stan turned to her and swore vile and violent threats, his hand still unable to make it to the gun.

"Get out of my family's house!" she screamed back. "You don't belong here! Get out, now!"

Jay grabbed her by the shoulder, pulled her back inside the door and locked it behind them.

"Okay, so that was both brave and impressive," he said. "You probably just saved us from being fired at. But now we've got to keep moving."

She didn't want to keep moving. She wanted to find a way, no matter how futile, to take a stand and protect her family home, even as she knew that Jay was right. They ran up a second flight of stairs and came out at the other end of the very same hallway they'd found themselves in two hours earlier.

They'd literally just been running around in a giant circle and, despite how hard they'd tried, hadn't come any closer to escaping.

Jay paced down the hallway, listening as if to figure out what direction the criminals were coming from. But she stopped for a moment and panted. Despair welled up inside her. Her sisters' door where they'd barricaded themselves behind earlier had been smashed in. The house was being destroyed bit by bit around her.

Help me, Lord! I don't know what to do or where to go. The verse she'd referenced at the bottom of her email to her sisters filled her mind. *From the end of the earth will I cry unto thee, when my heart is overwhelmed: lead me to the rock that is higher than I.*

According to Jay, her dad had told him that if they were ever in trouble to head to the attic. She hadn't listened to him then. But now, what other way was there to go but up? She glanced up at the ceiling hatch leading to the attic stairs. It was too high to reach without a ladder, and they didn't have time to find something to climb on. But there was more than one way to get up there.

"This way," she said. The door to her father's room lay open. She darted inside. The room had been tossed and the contents of her father's dresser and bookshelf had been scattered across the floor. But the huge four-poster bed that had been her parents sat in the middle of the room, and beside it the overstuffed pull-out chair that her father had slept in many nights, saying the bed felt wrong without her mom.

Jay rushed into the room behind her, closed the door and locked it behind him. "What are you doing?"

"We're heading to the attic," she said. "Like you first suggested. And since the hatch to the stairs is out in the hallway we're going to improvise."

She went over to the window, opened it and looked out, thankful the overhang of the dormer window shielded her from the rain. Below, her flashlight beams swung back and forth in the darkness. Jay leaned out the window beside her. His shoulder came in contact with hers.

"You're kidding," he said. "There's nothing to break our fall."

"We're not going to fall," she said. "You said yourself that Dad said if there was ever any trouble we should head to the attic. Not that I have any idea why. Don't worry, it'll be okay. I've done it before."

The door handle behind them turned and then it shook. Someone was trying to get in.

"Go!" Jay shouted. He ran across the

room and toward the door. "I'm right behind you."

"You'd better be." She slid her body out
the window and onto the ledge. Immediately
rain hit her anew. She gripped the shingles
of the dormer overhang above her. She whispered a prayer, grit her teeth and began to
climb.

The bedroom door was locked, but the
home invaders had already proved they
could rip a door down off its hinges if they
wanted to. Jay grabbed an overturned bookshelf and pushed it against the door, hoping it would buy them another few seconds
of time. Then he ran back to the window
where Leia had disappeared and looked out
in disbelief.

There was nothing there. No ladder, trel-
lis, rope or anything to hold on to. Just a
drop down to the ground below. His head
swam.

"Jay!" Her voice called down to him from
above but it was almost completely swallowed up by the raging storm. "I've made it.
It's okay. Just climb on top of the ledge over
the window and hoist yourself up."

He looked up toward the sound of her
voice and saw nothing but the dark and rainy

skies above. *I don't think I can do this.* He made sure the flashlight was still tucked firmly in his back belt loop. He glanced around the room in vain for anything that could be used as a rope in case they needed one to climb down, then yanked down the valance curtain and tied it over his shoulders.

Then he bent low and slowly stepped out onto the window ledge, crouching on the balls of his feet. His fingertips gripped the shingles of the dormer window overhang above him. Almost immediately one came off in his grasp, throwing his body backward into the thin air, with nothing but his toes on the ledge and the fingers on his other hand to keep him from falling. *Help me, God. I need You now!* Then his second hand found its grip on the window ledge again. He gasped a breath.

"You there?" Leia called down.

"Barely," he called back through gritted teeth. "I'm hanging out the window backward."

"Just hoist yourself up. There's a mini rooftop over the window."

Yup, he remembered.

He stood slowly, his body hanging backward at an uncomfortable angle as his arms spread wide so his hands could grip both sides of the small, peaked roof. Then he held his breath, let his feet leave the ledge and hoisted himself up on top of it, trying to tell himself this was no different than some of the strength exercises he'd done in training.

He scrambled up onto the ledge over the window, crouched on his feet and braced his hands against the slanted tile roof above him.

"Hey, I can see you!" Leia's warm voice floated toward him.

"Really?" he asked. Because he couldn't see a fool thing.

"Well, I can make out your general shape," she said. "All you have to do now is stand up and jump. The window will be only about six or eight inches above your head."

Right. Easy-peasy. He unfurled his legs slowly and walked his hands inch by inch up the slanted roof above him until he was half standing and half lying at an awkward angle against the shingles. And it hit him: this might actually be the most faith he'd ever placed in another human being.

"Just a few inches more," she said. "You're almost there."

He stretched his hands up over his head as far as his arms would go and felt her fingers as she reached down toward him. Her fingertips brushed his palms.

"See?" she said. She was panting slightly, and he wondered just how far she was leaning out the window. "You've got this. Now, the window ledge is maybe six to eight inches above you. I'm going to step back and you're going to jump up and grab it, okay?"

Confidence radiated through her voice as if she had absolutely no doubt that he was going to do exactly what she'd told him to. It made him feel stronger somehow. As if he didn't want to let her down.

"Got it," he called. "Step back!"

He tensed his legs and took a leap of faith up into the darkness. His left hand caught the window ledge and gripped it tight. His right swung out into nowhere, grasping ineffectually against the shingles as they pulled off under his grasp. Pain shot through his left arm from his fingertips to his shoulder as it was wrenched against suddenly holding up the full weight of his suspended body. And he became terrifyingly aware of just how few one-handed pull-ups he could do at the best of times. His muscles tensed as he pulled his body up. His feet scrambled ineffectually against the wet roof.

Help me, Lord. I'm going to fall.

Then he felt both of Leia's hands grab on to his forearm.

"It's okay," Leia said. "I've got you!"

Instinctively his other hand grabbed on to hers. He swung there, suspended, with his left hand still on the window ledge, both her hands on his left arm and his right hand gripping her hands as they held him.

"Don't worry," she said. "It's going to be fine. Just let go of the ledge and grab both my hands. I will help pull you up."

Let go? But what if she couldn't pull him up? What was she even bracing herself with? What if she wasn't strong enough to support his weight and they both fell?

"No," he said. "Let go of me and I'll pull myself up."

"Don't be ridiculous," she said. "You'll fall! Now come on. Trust me."

Vertigo swamped his brain. No, they couldn't do this. They weren't strong enough. He glanced up and saw her form leaning out the window above him.

"Jay!" Her voice broke. "Let me save you!"

What other choice did he have?

He set his jaw, whispered a prayer and dug his toes into the tiles so hard they ached. Then he let go. Instantly, he felt her hands grab ahold of his wrists. He grabbed hers back. For a second nothing happened—he just hung there suspended with their arms locked in each other's grasp. Then he felt his body begin to rise, inch by inch, as she leaned back and supported him, and they pulled him up together with their joint might. When his elbows scraped the window ledge, he felt the rain leave his head and back. He tumbled through the window and into the shelter of the attic. She let go of him and he of her, and they both collapsed on the floor, side by side, with their backs against the wall.

"Thank you," he said, the moment he found his voice.

"No problem," she replied, and he realized she was panting from exertion.

"You okay?"

"My arms have seen better days and my abs feel like I just planked for a week." She laughed. It was an infectiously happy sound he wished he could hear every day. "Told you that we could do it."

"You did," he said.

She stumbled to her feet. He followed and switched the flashlight on. The attic was maybe even smaller and plainer than he'd remembered it. It was slanted from floor to ceiling on both sides, forming two triangular-shaped brick walls at either end, only one of which had a window. He set the flashlight down and it rolled, sending cascading lights bouncing off the walls.

"Hang on, are you wearing one of Mom and Dad's curtains as a *cape*?" she asked. "If you know how to fly, you have to tell me."

He turned and looked at Leia. Her dark hair fell around her face in waves. Laughter lit up her violet eyes and slipped through the infectious smile curled on the corners of her lips. Suddenly his legs felt oddly weak.

She had no idea how incredibly beautiful she was or how his heart leaped every time he looked at her.

"Not a cape," he said. "I was actually looking for rope or something like that. I didn't have much time to think. If I had, I probably would've panicked. I think you might've saved my life."

"Maybe," Leia said lightly. "Either way, I'm really glad you're here in one piece."

Her arms slid around his neck in a quick and lighthearted hug. He hugged her back hard and gleefully swept her feet off the floor for a moment. But then somehow, as he set her feet back down and she pulled away from the hug, her hands still lingered there, linked right behind his neck. His hands found her back and his fingers splayed as if trying to hold every inch of her that he could.

"Don't even doubt I'll come through for you," she said. "Like it or not, we're in this together."

He liked it. Very much so.

"I don't know what to say," he admitted. "I'm sorry I underestimated you. Both how strong you were physically but also emotionally. I never imagined you'd still speak to me once you found out the truth, let alone help me."

She leaned forward and rested her forehead against his.

"You've rescued me, and I've rescued you," she said. "It's what people do when they care about each other. And I really did care about you, a lot."

"But how can you say you cared about me?" he asked. "You didn't *know* me. Any feelings you thought you had for me were based on a lie."

That had been the whole deal about living an undercover life. He had no siblings. His parents were gone. His only real friends would be in law enforcement. Nobody else would ever really know him.

"I knew you," she said. "Maybe not the details of your job or why you were here, but I didn't like you because you were a handyman. I liked how you thought about things and what you cared about. I liked how you treated me and respected my family. I liked how you responded to the world around you. I liked the man you were inside your undercover story. At least, until I realized you were the kind of man who could just turn off his feelings for me and throw what we had away."

He had to be that kind of man. He didn't have a choice. But that didn't mean he'd wanted to let her go. Not back then. Not right now.

The tip of her nose brushed his. Then their lips met. He tightened his arms around her; she held him closely and they kissed for a long moment, feeling happy and complete in a way that he hadn't in a very long time.

Even as a voice in the back of his mind told him that it was a mistake, that it would only happen this once and that he could never do it again or he'd risk losing everything else in his life that mattered.

EIGHT

For one long and breathtaking moment, Leia let herself kiss the only man her heart had ever longed for and never gotten over, blocking out the voice inside telling her that it would only be a matter of time before he pushed her away and broke her heart again. There was something that felt right about it, like she was where she was meant to be.

But it barely lasted a moment before they pulled apart again.

"You deserve so much better than a man who can never be honest with you," Jay said, "and who's always off living some under-cover life that his wife and kids can never be part of or even know about."

Was he even capable of truly falling in love with someone? Either way, she couldn't love a man incapable of loving her.

"You're right," she said and rolled her shoulders back. "I do, and after growing up with a father who kept secrets from me that's the last thing I want for my life."

And it was high time she remembered that. Jay had told her that he didn't want to fall in love or be in a relationship. He had talked about his feelings as if they were something he could easily push aside. She couldn't give Jay her heart. No matter how attractive he was or how much she might like him.

"You deserve to be able to chase your dreams and be the man you're meant to be without having a wife or family holding you back," Leia added. She wondered if he could hear the slight chill she felt creep into her voice.

"I'm just sorry I didn't find a way to tell you what was really going on," Jay said. "Maybe if I'd gone to your father, he might've agreed to fill you in on who I really was and what I was doing there."

"Or he'd have refused, stopped cooperating and kicked you off his property," Leia said. "My dad kept this secret from us for our entire lives. You couldn't have changed his mind. He was the most stubborn person I've ever met."

Suddenly hot and angry tears filled her eyes, and she didn't know if she was upset with her father, Jay, herself or all three.

"My own father didn't trust me," she went on. "He kept this from me my entire life. Dad spent all these hours homeschooling us, teaching us survival skills and telling us fairy tales. Even when he knew he was dying he didn't breathe a word of it and instead chose to take his secrets to the grave."

Then last summer, she'd developed romantic feelings for a man who was equally closed off and secretive. Thankfully their relationship had ended before it had gone much further. She stepped even farther away from Jay now, feeling that one brief, blissful moment they'd shared break into shards around their feet.

"Even this, being here in the attic with you, is a reminder of the fact that my dad kept me in the dark my whole life, just like you did last summer," she said. "Why was I forbidden from coming up here? There's nothing here. Just cobwebs and floorboards, with a hatch door leading back to the second-floor hallway. I can believe that my mom left my dad, went to Toronto, got close to Franklin Vamana and saw him kill someone. I believe my dad came to rescue her, that she made an anonymous call to police that wasn't followed up. And then my dad lived in fear for the rest of his life that Vamana was going to send men to kill me and my sisters in revenge, or something. All that actually makes sense to me. What I don't understand is why he didn't just tell me!"

"Maybe he wanted to protect you," Jay said. "Maybe he did something he was ashamed of or didn't want you to think less of him or your mom. People are complicated. I desperately missed my dad and wanted him to come back, no matter how many times well-meaning people tried to convince me I was better off without a recovering alcoholic in my life. My own mother never stopped loving him and believing he'd have never voluntarily left us. Maybe that's why I was so drawn to being an undercover officer. It meant I could change lives and help people, without getting too close to anyone and risking getting hurt like she did."

She turned away, picked up the flashlight from where he'd dropped it and swung it around the attic. It was so small it could barely be called a room; Jay's hideaway in the barn's loft was downright spacious by comparison.

"You weren't kidding when you said there was nothing here," she said. "I used to imagine my dad hid something valuable or special up here. But there really is nothing."

Jay chuckled self-consciously and ran his hand over the back of his neck.

"Yeah," he said. "I even felt around for loose floorboards and found nothing. It's not like your dad was about to give me permission to start tearing the place apart brick by brick."

"And yet when we were first on the run from the bad guys, your instinct was to come up here," she said.

"I don't know," he said. "Your dad's mind was pretty muddled by the end, but he just seemed convinced there was something up here."

He stepped closer and she felt her shoulders relax just by having him near. But she moved away. She didn't want to relax and couldn't afford to.

"Dad was an amazing storyteller," she said. "His stories were so detailed, and they were always the same ones, too. It's like he'd heard them somewhere and felt compelled to repeat them."

She could feel her hand tightening to a fist by her side. So she closed her eyes and prayed.

Lord, I'm frustrated. I know I should love my father and forgive him despite the choices he made. I know he loved me and I loved him. But I'm in trouble. I need my dad to help save me right now. But he's gone. So please, settle my heart and guide my mind.

"Did your dad ever tell a story about an attic?" Jay asked, like he was hazarding a wild guess.

"Yes, actually." Her eyes snapped opened. "Well, sort of. In one story, the four princesses find this tower with a triangular room at the very top. They discover that the brick wall is musical and they need to tap out a song on it to open a secret hatch."

Jay's eyes widened.

"How did the song go?" he asked. "Can you see what happens if you tap it out on the wall?"

"Really?" she asked. "That's a real long shot."

"I know," he said. "But I think we're all out of short shots right about now."

Wow, he was really suggesting she do it.

All right, then. She walked over to the wall and counted the bricks until she found the exact center one. She felt a chill lick her spine.

"I have to sing it," she said. "It's the only way I know."

"Got it," he said.

She placed her fingers on the cold dry

bricks and started tapping. "Right, right, right, up, up. Left, left, down, up, up."

Finally, she reached the final note and her fingers lingered on the last brick.

"Okay, this is it," she said. "Thank you for not laughing."

"I wouldn't dream of it," Jay said. He crossed over to the room and stood next to her. He pulled a small pocketknife from his pocket, flicked it open and gently pressed the tip of the blade in the mortar between the brick she'd landed on and the one beside it. She stepped back and watched him work. If there was anything bricked away within the wall, it had been there so long the mortar surrounding it was as old and set as the rest of it.

She took the flashlight and shone it at the space as he worked, carving the brick out of the wall on all sides. Finally he was done. He gripped it with his fingertips and pulled. It wiggled slightly in his hands, then slowly it came free from the wall with a low scraping sound.

"Whoa," Jay said. She shone the light into the dark hole behind. He reached for the flashlight. "Want to do the honors?"

"Thanks," she said. She reached in. The hole was dry, cool and only about six inches deep. She felt something soft yet rough under her fingers and pulled it out slowly.

It was a small burlap bag.

Jay stood back and watched, wordlessly, as she slowly unwrapped the canvas bag, reached inside and pulled out two items. The first was a metal storage box the size of a Bible with a safe-type combination keypad on the front. The other was a small photo album, the kind with printed four-by-six pictures in plastic sleeves.

His heart stopped. They'd found it—whatever *it* was that Leia's mother, Annie, presumably had hidden in the house. But what was it?

He waited as Leia punched a code in the keypad, half expecting the box to suddenly open. But it didn't. She frowned and tried another code, then another and another, until she'd hit at least twenty. Then she shook her head and held it out to him.

"Your guess is as good as mine," she said. "I've tried Mom's birthday, Dad's, mine and my sisters', along with their wedding anniversary and the date Mom died. I also tried converting all of our names and middle names to numbers, and all his favorite Bible verses."

"What about the name of that imaginary land he told stories about," Jay asked.

"Cymbafalls?" she asked. She spelled it out slowly on the keypad, then futilely jiggled the handle. "Nope, doesn't open. You want to try?"

"Sure, but I doubt I'll do any better," he said. He took it from her and started entering all the dates and names he could think of related to Franklin Vamana and the Phantom Killer case, but nothing budged the lock.

She turned the small book of pictures over in her hand.

"I haven't seen an actual photo album like this in years," she said. "My dad had a really big one with all our family photos in it. You know the kind where you stab your fingers on the little clear sleeves when you slide the picture in and then they get stuck in there and meld to the plastic?"

She flipped through the pages and, as he watched, her smile faded.

"What is it?" he asked.

"Baby pictures," she said. Her frowned deepened. "*My* baby pictures to be exact."

She tilted the page so he could see it. There sat a tiny infant, wrapped in a blanket, no more than a few days old in her mother's arms. Walter stood in the background, leaning over her shoulder, grinning ear to ear.

"It's odd to see them looking so young," Jay said. "They're younger than we are."

"No, what's odd is the Easter basket with my name on it on the table," she said, and pointed. "And the fact there's a copy of this exact same picture on the family album with the basket cropped out."

"What am I missing?" Jay said. "So they made you a basket for Easter when you were tiny."

She pressed her lips together and didn't answer. But he could tell from the worry in her eyes that whatever it meant it wasn't good. She kept flipping through pictures. There was baby Leia in Annie's arms standing outside the family farmhouse while purple crocuses poked through the snow. In another, she was in Walter's arms and he was holding a bouquet of daffodils in his gloved hand.

"When were these taken?" she asked. Something urgent rose in her voice. "Tell me. What month is this?"

"I don't know," he said. "I have no idea."

"Yes, you do," she said. "You grew up in Ontario. When was this?"

"April, I'm guessing," he said. The whole

thing felt like a trick answer with very high stakes. "Maybe the Easter picture was taken sometime around the end of March, depending when the holiday was that year. Snow like that could be April. It's very rare we have any snow as late as May. And I'd say those flowers definitely bloom sometime around then. I think the purple ones bloom first and daffodils are around Easter. Why?"

She didn't answer. Instead, her shoulders dropped and her hands fell to her sides. He tried to gently pry the photo album from her fingers, but her grip had almost frozen around it. Her chin began to shake and he watched as tears filled her eyes.

"Leia," he said softly.

She shook her head.

"If I start to cry…" she said. Her voice quavered. "Please don't hug me. I don't want to be held right now."

"Got ya," he said. "But if you need a hug, or if there's anything else I can do, let me know. I'm here."

"Thank you," she said.

As she turned and he saw her face, he realized with a jolt that anger filled her face, mingling with the grief.

"My birthday is in June," she said slowly, as if making her way across a bridge that might collapse at any moment. "Late June. But I was born at home in this very farmhouse. My dad delivered me. He said it was because I came quickly and there was no time to get Mom to the hospital, and maybe that's true. But I know that meant they traveled into Kilpatrick one day in December to register my birth with the province and get my birth certificate. When it's a home birth, you're allowed to wait awhile."

Tears swamped her eyes. She blew out a long breath, as if trying to calm and settle her voice.

"But I wasn't born in June, was I?" she asked, her voice cracking. "My parents lied about my birthday. I was really born in late March or early April probably. Not ten months after my parents got married but seven or eight." She shook her head, and tears rolled from her eyes. "Because my dad's not really my dad, is he? Because my mom was already pregnant with me when she ran away in the middle of the night, when my dad… I mean, when Walter came to save her. Because my real father is Franklin Vamana."

NINE

"You can't know that," Jay said, the words flying from his mouth as the full implication of what she was saying hit him. "It's possible you were born early, your parents met up secretly that summer or the pictures are misleading."

"I know," Leia said. Her voice rose. "But think, Jay. What makes the most sense? What fits all the evidence? I don't look anything like my sisters. They're all blonde, and I've got this really dark hair. I've always known I didn't look like I belonged, and you said yourself Franklin's mother had purple eyes. My father was paranoid of someone coming to kidnap us. Doesn't that make sense if he knew I was actually another man's child? They changed my birthday. They only went after Franklin anonymously, and my father took these secrets to the grave. He loved me and never wanted me finding out that my biological father was a serial killer." Her shoulders rose and fell. "He was faithful to the man he was to the very end and did it to protect me."

Jay swallowed hard. "For all you know, he promised your mother never to let anyone find out."

She slid the photo album inside her pocket and ran both her hands through her hair.

"Maybe," she said. "Probably. I can believe that. But that still means my biological father is a criminal, and the man who raised me like a dad lied to me my whole life."

Not to mention, she'd almost gotten involved with me. *A man incapable of giving her the love and life she'd deserved.*

A deep ache filled Jay's chest. Everything inside him wanted to gather her up into his chest, hold her to him, kiss away the tears from her eyes and take away the pain. Even though he knew he couldn't.

"Look, it's your secret," he said. "I can't speak for whatever might be hiding in that box we still can't open. But the pictures of you as a baby are nobody's business but yours, and you don't have to tell anyone if you don't want to. As for your hypothesis about your birth father, you can't even prove it without getting Franklin Vamana to agree to a DNA test. And if he refused, that could be an expensive legal battle you couldn't even afford. What we talked about here doesn't have to leave this room. Nobody has to know."

"But *we'll* know," Leia said. "I'll always know that I'm not the person I grew up thinking I was. And you'll always know that I might be the biological daughter of the man who you've been chasing. The man who might've murdered your father."

Something tightened in Jay's chest like a cold fist gripping his heart. He crossed his arms.

"I will never hold that against you or think anything different about you because of that," he said.

"You sure?" Leia asked. "Because you wouldn't be human if you didn't. You told me you're good at shutting down emotions you don't want to feel. Do you really want to add this to the list of things you won't feel?"

Yes, he did, and he would. He had to. Something this terrible was just too much to bear. To his surprise, she stepped toward him until her body bumped lightly against his crossed arms.

"Would it be okay if I got that hug from you now?" she asked. "Thanks for respecting the fact I really needed to process this a bit first, but now I think I could really use one."

"Of course," he said. And yet his arms felt stiff as they unfolded, as if reluctant to move. As she stepped into his chest and wrapped her arms around him, his own hands didn't seem to fit comfortably against her back anymore, as if they were two broken pieces of pottery with the edges so chipped that they no longer quite matched up and fit together. "I'm not saying it won't be hard for me to forget but I'll work at it."

"I don't want you to," she said, and pulled back. "If you go through life denying your feelings where does it stop? I don't like knowing this about me. It feels disgusting, and I can't imagine anyone ever choosing to love the daughter of the Phantom Killer. You deserve so much better than that. But an ugly truth is still true."

"Hey," Jay said. He reached for her face and tilted it up until her eyes met his. "Listen to me. This doesn't have to define you. You are brilliant and beautiful. You're kind, caring and one of the bravest people I know. Anyone would be unbelievably blessed to have you as their friend, let alone anything more than that."

"Thank you," she said. "You're amazing,

too. But we can't keep holding each other like this, and once we get out of here I can't be all alone with you this way ever again. You know that, right? You've been honest about the fact you don't want a romantic relationship with me. I am a threat to your career and your future. And I need to figure out who I even am and I can't do that with someone who's not committed to being there for me."

"Yeah," he said slowly. He rolled his jaw slowly, trying to quell the bitter taste in his mouth. "You're right. I don't like it and I'm going to miss you, but you're right."

"Turns out we're a really good team when it comes to dealing with a crisis like this," she said. "But I don't want to live in a moment like this forever. I still want to throw myself into my job, my schooling and being a family with my sisters and baby niece. I want to create a happy and meaningful life and live it to the fullest."

And find a man capable of loving her and being there for her, the way he never would.

Sudden screams rose from the window beneath them and he watched as all the color drained from Leia's face. The sound of a small baby crying out in fear mingled with the sound of a woman bravely telling the criminals who were now shouting and swearing at her that they were not to lay a hand on her child.

"Sally and Mabel are back early!" she said. He reached out his hand to steady her as he watched her legs begin to crumple beneath her. "And Vamana's goons have them!"

A wave of dread washed over Leia's heart with so much strength and power that for a moment Jay's supportive hold on her arms was the only thing that kept her from crumpling to the floor. She'd failed at every turn. She hadn't managed to escape, to get an email message out to the outside world or warn her sister not to come home early with her precious baby girl. Leia closed her eyes and tried to pray. But fear beat around her on all sides, filling her heart and mind with the worst possible questions, thoughts and images of what could happen next. She was drowning in the terror of what was and what could be. Then she heard the soft voice of Jay praying and asking God to help them; it broke in at the side of her mind, like a lighthouse beam calling her home.

She opened her eyes.

"Hey," Jay said firmly. He pulled her

away from the window. "As I'm sure your father taught you, the first few minutes after any kidnapping is the most crucial for survival and escape. We've got to act quickly. So, I need you to focus for me and tell me how we're going to rescue your sister."

Her eyes widened. "I don't know."

"Yes," he said, and somehow his tone softened slightly without losing any of the grit. "You have a whole lot of knowledge about both your sister and this house in your mind. You're probably the utmost expert on it. So, let's figure this out together and then take action."

"I can't," she said. A sob slipped her lips. Her head shook. "Maybe at another time or another day. But right now I'm exhausted. Both my body and emotions feel like they've been put through the ringer."

"Yes, you can," Jay said. "Please, Leia, I need you."

But I don't even know where to start.

He closed his eyes and she watched as silent prayers moved on his lips.

"Tell me, what's the first thing Sally does after being kidnapped," he said. "Does she fight? Try to escape?"

"No," she said automatically. "Not in the way anyone would think. Sally is smart in a very logical and almost mechanical way. She's impossible to play board games with because she's always thinking eight steps ahead. She'd try to find a way to maneuver herself out of the situation. I mean that literally. She'll keep them talking to make them think she's cooperative. She'll try to manipulate them into putting her somewhere that she can easily escape from and keep them from locking her up too tight. Right now, she'll be focused on keeping Mabel safe."

"So, let's say she's succeeding," Jay said. "Where are they keeping her?"

"Main floor," she said. "Maybe living room. Somewhere with a lot of exits."

"Okay," he said, and she watched as the slightest glimmer of a determined smile crossed his lips. He eased his hands off her arms and she realized her legs felt strong enough to stand. "Any other strengths?"

"She's a brilliant mechanic," Leia said. "She met her estranged husband at the garage where she was working and ended up joining the pit crew for this car race he was into. She'd have figured out what was wrong with your truck much faster than you."

"Anything else?"

Lord, my heart is overwhelmed. Lead me to the rock that is higher than I.

"She can navigate this place in the dark even better than I can," she said.

"So, we cut the power," Jay said. "I'm guessing there's a fuse box and breakers in the basement."

"Yes, but we don't need them," she said. "This house is so old it still has an aboveground power line attached to the side of the house at the roof. It's really weak, too. A tree branch falling on it, a windstorm and heavy snow or ice will bring it down no problem. We have at least one power outage every year thanks to downed power lines. All we need is for one of us to climb across the roof to where the power line attaches to the house and take it down."

"And considering that will then plunge the house into darkness," Jay said, "I should be the one who takes the power line down once you're in position."

He looked slightly queasy at the thought.

"Just tie the valance curtain to a ceiling beam or around a loose floorboard and slide along the roof on your bottom like you're sledding down an icy hill without a toboggan," she said. "The drainage pipe should stop you from careening over the edge, but if not you'll have the curtain for backup. Then it's just a matter of downing the power."

"You make it sound so simple," he said.

"Do you want to switch?" she asked.

"No," he said. "Your sister needs you and you know the house better than me."

"Now, once the power is out," she said, "we'll still need to create a diversion."

"Oh, I think that'll be pretty much covered," Jay said. "If I succeed in tearing down the electrical line it'll be sizzling, sparking and giving off a very pretty fireworks show. In a storm like this it'll be even more noticeable."

"Not to mention that it could kill you," Leia said, "even if it's not giving off a pretty light show."

"I'll be safe," he said. "I promise. You stay safe, too."

"I will," she said.

"You'd better."

His voice deepened and an emotion swam in his dark eyes that she couldn't risk letting herself put into words. He cared about her, and she cared about him despite every single thing that had happened since he'd come into her life. She was endlessly thankful that he'd been around. But caring wasn't the same as being in love. And it wasn't enough to build a future on.

"Do you want to take my gun?" he asked.

"No, you're still a better shot than I am," she said, "despite a few good rounds I got off at the range. Plus, I'll be completely in the dark and with a baby."

"Fair enough," he said. "At least take my knife and my truck keys. There's also a tiny flashlight on the chain. If Sally can get it running and I've completely disappeared, then I expect you to run without me, and get her and the baby to safety."

"Will do," she said. "Thank you."

He handed her the knife still attached to the key chain. She took it and their fingers lingered against each other for a long time, neither of them seeming to be ready to pull away.

"Stay safe, okay?" she said. "Your story is not allowed to have a tragic ending. You're going to stop the bad guys, unmask the serial killer and save the day."

Maybe one day he'd even open up his heart and get the girl, although it wouldn't be her.

"Got it," he said.

She tucked his key chain inside her jacket along with the locked mystery box and photo album. Leia leaned forward and brushed a quick kiss over Jay's cheek. Then she turned around, climbed out the window and slid back down the roof.

TEN

Jay's heart sat well and truly lodged in his throat as he watched the ease with which Leia slid down the slippery roof tiles and landed on the dormer window ledge over her parents' bedroom window just as smoothly as a child on a plastic slide in the playground. She gave a little wave and then slipped around the side of the ledge, back through the window and was gone.

Had she forgotten there was a hatch in the floorboards that opened onto a perfectly good but narrow ladder leading down to the second floor? Or had she assumed that sliding down the roof would be safer, faster or both?

Either way, it was now his turn. He crouched down low, eased the attic hatch open an inch and looked down. Ross stood directly below him. If he dropped through, he'd land right on top of him. He eased the hatch shut again. Looked like he really was going out the window again, which would be the most direct route, after all, considering the power line was attached to the outside of the house.

He pressed his hand against his chest and felt his heart beating through it. It was ironic. For years he'd worried that his less than perfect inner ear would be what would keep him from fulfilling his dream of being an undercover cop. Then he'd conquered every physical exam and training exercise with flying colors and it had turned out his fear was unfounded. Only then to be blindsided by the realization the problem might actually be his imperfect heart.

Did Leia really think that he'd think less of her because of who her biological father was? Or that he somehow deserved *better*? He was the one who wasn't good enough for her.

And right now, he was going to do everything in his power to rescue her, her sister and the baby, starting with taking the power out. He took the wet valance, ripped it into three vertical strips and braided it into a rope. Then he tied it to the ceiling beam closest to the window, wrapped it twice around his hand and climbed out. Immediately his feet slipped on the slanting shingles, turning his attempted controlled slide into a fast luge down the roof. His feet hit the drainpipe, then his body lurched forward, dangling face-first over the backyard for a moment, before he yanked back on the makeshift rope and managed to land sprawled, but seated, on the corner of the roof.

Well, then, looked like he wasn't about to win any awards for style, but he'd stuck the landing. The black electrical wires stretched out beneath him as thick as a tug-of-war rope. On the plus side, he could probably be able to take it down from body weight alone. Unfortunately, that might also mean getting electrocuted and/or falling to his death.

He waited a long moment and scanned the ground below for flashlight beams and saw one that appeared and disappeared around the far side of the house. Faint light glowed from the house's main floor. Ironically, he was somehow feeling less afraid and more confident than anyone had any right to be in this situation, and the reason for it was Leia. She made him feel strong and capable in a way he'd never felt before, and it eased that pesky voice of doubt that forever tormented the corners of his mind. *And I'm going to do everything I can to make sure she gets out of here safely.* Which meant he couldn't afford to overthink things and be afraid.

Something rustled in a tree to his right. Startled, he gripped the edges of the roof for a moment. Then he watched as Moses the cat burst from the leaves, ran down a branch and then leaped past him onto the roof. The cat ran down the edge of the roof and then disappeared through the same window that Leia had entered.

Well, that was one way to do it.

He scanned the tree. It towered high above the house past the electrical wires, with thick branches at least six or seven inches wide. Several of the branches were definitely large enough to take the power down, yet also thin enough he could probably break them off by sheer force alone. Something told him that Leia or her sisters would just hop off the roof onto the branch without thinking twice. But he waited a long moment, praying, before raising to his feet and leaping.

Help me, Lord!

His body hit the tree, and as both feet landed on the branch he'd been aiming for, he instinctively grabbed ahold of the trunk with both hands for support. So far so good.

"Hey!" Ross shouted below him. "Who's there?"

Before Jay could even exhale, the man below opened fire, peppering the tree with bullets and shredding the leaves around him. The tree shook and swayed from the impact. Jay pressed his body against the trunk and wrapped one arm around it tightly. His head swam as vertigo swept over him, threatening to send him falling. Slowly Jay pulled his gun from his holster. Clearly Ross with his wild aim couldn't see Jay, but unfortunately that meant Jay had no idea where he was, either. He clenched his jaw and readied his gun, praying for guidance on where to fire. Then, in the chaos exploding around him, he had a sudden moment of clarity.

The only thing that mattered right now was taking the power out.

He turned toward the house, raised his gun toward the bracket holding the electrical wires to the house and fired. He heard it clang in the darkness. He loaded the next bullet into the chamber and fired again. This time he heard a snap, then watched as the electrical cables fell from the house and down into the brush beneath him. Voices shouted, and sparks flew on the ground like a volcano trying to spark.

The farmhouse lights went dark.

* * *

Leia was crouched low behind the living room sofa when the lights went out, with her eyes trained on where her sister stood in the kitchen. On the plus side, Sally wasn't tied up; she was only being watched by one guard, Willie, and had somehow talked him into letting her use the stove-top kettle, presumably to make a baby bottle for Mabel. On the bad side, Leia didn't actually see the baby.

She leaped the moment the house went dark, charging at the man holding her sister at gunpoint, only to hear a resounding clang followed by a thud. Leia switched the flashlight on, somehow knowing exactly the scene she'd see.

Willie was down on the kitchen floor knocked out cold. Sally stood over him with her waist-length blond hair tied back in a braid and the kettle clutched in her hand, still steaming from the water she'd been boiling. Sally turned toward Leia, kettle raised as if to strike her, too, and Leia watched as relief swept over her sister's body.

"Leia!" A sob slipped from Sally's lips as she dropped the kettle on the table and hugged Leia fiercely.

"You okay?" Leia asked. She hugged her sister back, feeling tears filling her own eyes. *Thank You, God, that my sister's okay.*

"Yes, but they've got Mabel." Sally pulled out of her arms as quickly as they'd embraced. Fear pooled in her eyes. "But men with guns surrounded me the moment I got out of the car and forced me into the house. Mabel wouldn't stop screaming, so this young guy with brown curls said he was a dad and that he'd walk her around while I made a bottle."

"Listen to me." Leia took her shoulders. "It's going to be okay. They don't want to hurt us. They're just looking for something. I'll explain later. But Jay is here, too, and he's going to help us find Mabel and escape. I'll take the front and you take the back. Can we use your car?"

"No," Sally said. She shook her head. "They took my keys, phone and wallet."

"Take Jay's keys," Leia said, pressing them into her sister's hand. "His truck is in the garage and we'll meet there. They disabled his engine somehow."

"Okay…okay…" Sally said, like her brain was stalling.

Sympathy swept over Leia. She'd had hours to try and figure out what was going on and Sally had just been thrust into it. She grabbed her sister's hand. "Lord, help us find Mabel, get the truck running and escape from here. We are overwhelmed and scared. Be our Rock right now."

Then she let go and watched as fresh strength filled Sally's eyes. Leia bent down and checked the man on the floor; he was both breathing and groaning.

"Did I kill him?" Sally asked.

"No," Leia said. "Also, don't feel too bad for hitting him. He tried to shoot the cat."

The sisters hugged again. Sally switched off the small flashlight. Leia scooped up the handgun that Willie had dropped, slipped the safety on and took it with her.

She moved through the darkened living room, barely able to see even the faintest outlines and shadows of the furniture. She burst through the front door and onto the front porch. A figure suddenly loomed in front of her in the darkness. Instinctively she raised the weapon, planning to coldcock him in the face. But before she could strike she felt a warm hand clamp over her mouth and another direct her gun down and away from him as he pushed her back against the farmhouse wall.

"It's okay," Jay's rough voice whispered in her ear. His breath caressed her face. "We just can't make a sound. People are patrolling the area looking for me."

She nodded and he pulled his hand away from her mouth. A flashlight moved past them in the darkness as someone ran past. The light disappeared again.

"Why are they looking for you?" she whispered, leaning in so close that she felt her mouth brush his ear. He shivered.

"I fell from a tree because Ross was shooting at me," he said. "Thankfully I managed to take the power out and avoided getting electrocuted by the live wire, so overall I consider it a win. Where's your sister and the baby?"

"Sally took Willie out with a kettle," she said. "Unfortunately, someone took Mabel for a walk."

Tension rose through Jay's shoulders so swiftly she felt it move into her own body.

"We'll find her," he said. "I promise. I'm hopeful they won't hurt the baby. It sounds like they have very specific orders they're following."

"I hope so, too," she admitted. *Please, Lord, keep the baby safe.*

"What did he look like?" he asked.

"Young with brown curls, and he said he was a father."

"That would be Ben." Jay peeled away from her and took a deep breath. "Let's go find the baby and get out of here. I hate to say this but I suggest we split up. There's a lot of outdoor ground to cover, and I'm guessing that's what you agreed with Sally, too."

She nodded. "It is. Sally's gone to the garage."

"You head toward the barn, then, and I'll head toward the road," Jay said.

It was the right thing to do. Splitting up to cover the most ground was the fastest and smartest way to find the baby, and right now that was all that mattered.

"Thanks for not shooting me," Jay added. Even in the darkness she could hear the smile in his voice and knew how much she'd miss it. "Where'd you finally get a gun?"

"Took it off Willie after Sally hit him with the kettle," she said. "And I wasn't going to shoot you. The range was too close, and the safety was on. I was going to coldcock you with it."

Jay chuckled softly. "That's my girl."

"Thank you, Cop Boy."

"You just stay safe, okay?" His lips brushed the top of her head and she heard him whisper a prayer for her safety. "See you soon."

He took off running into the darkness. Leia inhaled a deep breath and prayed, then she started toward the barn. Almost immediately she missed having Jay by her side. Just that small encounter for a few brief moments had made her feel stronger than she had before. The barn came into view, then she heard a faint sound coming from it. A baby was crying.

She ran for it, pelting up the slope of grass toward the barn. Her heart ached with every step, praying that she'd find her little niece okay. The barn door was open a foot; she stopped, raised her weapon and stepped inside.

A young man with wet curls sticking up wildly in all directions spun toward her. He was holding a lit cigarette in one hand and a handgun in the other. An opened bottle of vodka sat near him on a bale of hay. Behind him she could see tiny Mabel sitting in her car seat on another bale in the back of the barn, her face scrunched in tears as she wailed.

"Hands up, Ben!" Leia shouted, and aimed the gun between his eyes with both hands. "I don't want any trouble. Just step away from the baby and let me take her. Also, put out your cigarette. What are you thinking, smoking and drinking in a barn near a baby?"

"That's why I set her down over there!" Ben yelled. He seemed to be more agitated about the smoking comment than the fact she was training a gun on him. "And I was blowing the smoke away from her."

"I don't care what you told yourself," Leia said. "Just let me take the baby and go."

He hesitated, and suddenly she wondered what would happen if he didn't let her leave with the baby. Sure, she knew she was a good enough shot to take him out; her grip on the gun was steady, while he was only holding the gun with one shaking hand. But did she have it in her heart to hurt someone? Or even kill someone? She'd never in a million years imagine that she did. But that was before she'd learned she probably had the blood of a serial killer pulsing through her veins. *Lord, I need Your wisdom. I don't even know who I am anymore.*

Then she remembered the words that Jay had hurriedly spoken to her under the shelter of the porch roof.

"You're a father, right, Ben?" she asked, using his name in the hopes it would help her make a connection. "When you volunteered to take the baby for a walk it was to protect her, wasn't it?"

Ben took a swig of vodka from the bottle with the same hand that was holding the cigarette and then dropped it back on the hay.

His hands shook so much for a moment she wasn't sure if he was at more risk of accidentally firing the gun, knocking over his alcohol or dropping the cigarette into a bale of hay. And suddenly her heart ached; he was terrified.

Mabel's cries grew. It would be so easy for her to just shoot him right now, take the baby and run. She'd grown up asking herself what she'd actually do if she ever came face-to-face with an actual "bad guy" like the ones in her father's fairy tales. He'd always taught her to "act justly, show mercy and walk humbly" as went one of his other favorite verses from the Bible.

But Walter hadn't been her real father, had he? He was someone who'd lied to her and kept secrets about who she was for her whole life—even letting her believe she was a few weeks younger than she actually was. And she was supposed to let his teaching guide her choices now?

Help me be true to the person You've made me to be.

"I don't smoke or drink around my kid," Ben said. "His mother doesn't like it."

Again, not the point. But in her work at legal aid, as she trained to be a lawyer, she'd learned that scared and broken people sometimes got their minds hung up on the wrong things.

"I get that, Ben," she said. "You want to be a good dad and have a relationship with your own baby. Just like I want to be a good aunt and take my niece somewhere safe. In fact, that's the only thing I care about right now."

The face of her father's beaming smile as he held her as a newborn baby filled her mind. That look of pride and love had never once dimmed from his eyes every time he'd looked at her over her entire life. There'd never been a moment she'd doubted he loved her and her mother. Had her father been blinded by love? Had he carried this painful burden alone his entire life, in secret, out of his own misguided desire to care for her the best he could. The sound of her niece crying and her tearstained face made her feel like she'd do anything in the entire world to protect her. Maybe that's what she needed to hold on to, to forgive the man who raised her.

"How do you know my name?" Ben's voice shook. He took another drink. Bright orange ash fell from his cigarette.

"You had a tussle with my friend Jay earlier tonight," she said. Jay hadn't hesitated to show Ben mercy. "You told him you had legal problems? Well, I work for legal aid on King Street East. Let me take the baby and go. Then come find me when this is all done, and I'll do whatever I can to make sure you get the help you need. I promise."

She took a leap of faith, lowered the gun and put the safety back on. Then she started walking toward the baby, keeping her eyes firmly on Ben.

"You're not going to shoot me," she said. "It takes a lot to kill someone for the first time and I don't think that's you. I think you're just caught up in something way over your head. My friend Jay could've killed you, but he didn't. So, I'm asking you to pay him back and let me take the baby now."

The faint smell of burning hay rose from where Ben's ash kept falling. Mumbled swear words spilled from his lips like he was berating himself. But he didn't stop her. He picked up the vodka again, took a swig and set it down. The bottle slipped off the edge of the bale, fell to the ground and spilled its contents.

She reached the crying baby, fought the urge to pull her out of her car seat and instead gently wiped the tears from Mabel's eyes. "It's going to be okay, baby girl," she whispered. "I promise."

All she had to do was walk back out of the barn, past Ben and out into the night.

"Hey!" Suddenly Stan's angry voice filled the space. "What's going on here?"

She dropped to the floor, pulling Mabel down with her and clutching her to her chest.

"I… I didn't want to hurt the woman or the baby!" Ben said. He turned and pointed the gun at Stan. "I just want to go. I won't tell anyone. I promise. I just want to go."

"Nobody goes anywhere until this is done," Stan said.

Without warning he fired at the younger man and his bullet caught Ben on the shoulder.

Ben screamed in pain. The cigarette fell from his hand, hitting the vodka on the floor; instantly it sprung alight, sending a wall of flames rushing up the dry hay and spreading up the walls.

Leaving her and Mabel trapped in the back of the burning barn.

ELEVEN

Jay pelted through toward the barn as bright orange flames licked out of the windows and up at the sky. Suddenly he heard a smooth motor behind him, and his body was swamped in the glare of headlights. Instinctively, he braced himself to roll away from the wheels when he heard a horn honk and looked back to see his own truck swerve to a stop behind him.

Sally stuck her head out the window. "Get in!"

He ran to the passenger's side and leaped in. "You fixed my truck."

"I did," Sally said. She gritted her teeth and kept driving the moment the door clicked shut. "Long story short, somebody cut a bunch of wires, so I spliced them back together with a pocket knife and duct tape. Have you seen Leia or Mabel?"

"Leia was heading to the barn," he said.

Her face paled. "That's where I think Mabel is, too. It's faint but I think I can hear her crying."

He lowered the window and listened. For a moment he couldn't hear anything but the rumble of the engine and the crackle of flames devouring the barn from the inside. But as they raced closer, he could hear faint voices coming from the burning barn. Mabel was crying and Leia was screaming for help.

"What's going on?" Sally asked.

"I'm an undercover cop," Jay said. "Your father was an informant. Your sister can fill you in on the rest."

"So, you're back together?" Sally asked.

"What? No." Jay's mouth gaped. "You knew about that?"

"Why else do you think my sisters and I rehired you?"

He didn't have an answer to that. "If anything happens to me, promise you'll get Leia to safety, no matter what."

"I promise."

They reached the barn and he leaped out, even before Sally had fully engaged the brakes. Heat hit him like a wave as he yanked the barn door open. Smoke filled his vision.

"Leia!" he shouted. "Can you hear me!"

"I'm here in the back with Mabel," she shouted. "We're trapped and can't get out. Rain's coming in from the window above me and that's keeping the fire away for now. Ben was shot by Stan, but I think he made it out alive. I don't know where Stan is now."

He thanked God Leia and the baby were alive. But they couldn't stay there forever. *Help us, God!* He took a step forward in the smoke, only to feel the heat push him back. He turned to Sally.

"They're trapped in the back by a window," he said.

"Got it," Sally said. She rolled the windows up and revved the engine.

He leaped back and watched as she drove his truck through the partially opened barn door and into the flames. Wood splintered and fell. A flame-covered beam fell and smashed against the back of his truck. He held his breath for the longest, most excruciating moment of his life, praying that Leia and the baby were okay. There in the glare of the truck's headlights he watched as Leia's silhouette emerged from the dense smoke, holding the car seat in her hands. She climbed into the truck and it charged backward out of the barn.

And in that moment Jay knew that no matter how long and what kind of life he had, he'd never care about another person as much as his heart longed to know Leia was safe. He just prayed that God would lead her to a husband who'd protect her and take care of her as much as Jay longed to.

He stood far back as the truck emerged backward from the flames. Sally spun it around and hit the brakes. Jay's eyes met Leia's through the window. She rolled it down and he could hear the hardy cry of Mabel wailing. Tears of thanksgiving to God pressed unshed against his eyes.

"Told you Sally would get it running!" she shouted, a smile filling her soot-and-tearstained face. "Come on, get in! We've got to go!"

He ran for the truck, joy filling his heart. It was all going to be okay. They had wheels, they were all together and they were going to get to safety and call for help. They'd find a way to open the hidden box. It was almost over.

A figure rose from the truck bed like a phantom, his body so covered in soot and hay that for a moment Jay didn't recognize him. It was Stan. He raised his weapon at the glass window at the back of the cab and pointed it directly at the women's heads. "Get out! Both of you! Now!"

Jay couldn't risk shooting the man from behind. If he fell and his finger twitched, even a little, his bullet would fly right through the glass, hitting Leia, Sally or the baby. Jay ran and leaped onto the back of the truck.

"Hey!" Jay shouted. "Leave them alone!"

Stan spun toward him and fired, the bullet flying over his head as Jay charged. Jay caught him around the stomach in a football tackle, bracing himself as the older man rained down furious blows to his head. Stan caught him in his bad ear and a high-pitched whine filled Jay's head and nausea swept over him. More shouting filled the air as the two men wrestled in the back of the truck for control; it sounded like Willie and Ross were now running in for backup. Through the chaos, he heard Leia's side door open.

Jay banged his fist on the back of the truck.

"No, Leia!" he shouted. "Drive! Go! Get help! Now! I need you safe!"

The truck lurched forward. Suddenly he was falling, rolling and tumbling off the truck, still locked in a grip with Stan. The sound of Leia shouting his name filled his ears, fading on the wind as the truck drove away into the night.

Ross and Willie reached his side and aimed their guns down at his head as Stan scrambled to his feet and joined them, leveling a final kick to Jay's gut. He was down on the ground and surrounded on all sides. But Jay's eyes fixed on the fading headlights until they disappeared. Then his eyes rose to the huge bonfire of burning wood and flame that had once been the barn, taking all of his notes and wall of research photos along with it.

He felt his body collapse onto the ground like a dancing car-lot balloon man when someone cut off the air keeping it up. It was all over, for him and for his case. But at least Leia was safe.

"We have to go back," Leia said. She gripped the door handle so tightly her fingers ached. She looked at her sister as she navigated through the night, pushing the truck to almost twice the speed limit. "Sally, they'll kill him."

"I know," Sally said. "He made me promise not to stop until I had you somewhere safe, and I can't return until I get Mabel to safety. But we'll figure this out together, and if you want to go back for him you've got my full support."

Leia slumped against the seat as the fatigue and pain she'd been ignoring all night finally caught up with her. Sally was right. Simply running back into a swarm of criminals with guns would get her nowhere.

She glanced at Mabel. Somehow, due to the soothing sound of her mother's voice and the moving vehicle, she'd fallen asleep in her car seat again.

"Tell me what's happening," Sally said. "Then we can figure it out together. All Jay told me was that he was an undercover cop, Dad was somehow an informant and you two aren't back together."

"Back together?" Leia blinked. "You knew about us?"

"We all did," Sally said. "Not the full extent of whatever was going on between you last summer, but the looks you exchanged made it pretty clear. Quinn, Rose and I went to Dad together and told him to make it clear Jay had his blessing to pursue a relationship."

"But he said no?" Leia guessed.

"Yup," Sally said. She cast her sister a quick side glance and a slight smile before turning her attention back to the road.

"That's why we were all so insistent about hiring him back. We thought you two could patch it up."

"Oh, I had no idea." Leia felt like the stuffing had been knocked out of her. "Well, next time talk to me instead of playing matchmaker."

They lapsed into silence as the truck drove deeper into the night. Leia felt inside her jacket. The locked box and baby photo album were still there. How could she even explain everything to Sally? Logically, the way Sally would. She took a deep breath.

"Simple facts first," Leia said. "Our top priority is calling the cops and getting them to storm the farmhouse and rescue Jay. As he told you, Jay is an undercover police officer investigating a cold-case serial killer called the Phantom Killer. We need to avoid revealing that about him, though, if at all possible, so that he maintains his cover. Dad contacted him last year saying there might be evidence hidden in the house that proved the serial killer was Franklin Vamana."

Sally's eyes widened. "Of Vamana Enterprises? Brother to Esther Vamana of the Indigo Iris makeup empire?"

"Yup," Leia said. "Criminals showed up tonight, cut the phone lines, took down the cell tower and ransacked the house, looking for something connected to Vamana. I tried using the old computer to email you, Quinn and Rose, but one of the criminals shot up the machine."

"Sorry he beat me to it," Sally said. "I hate that thing."

"Jay and I found this locked box hidden behind a brick in the attic," Leia went on. She pulled it out of her jacket and held it up. "So far we haven't been able to open it."

"Did you try Mom's birthday?" Sally asked.

"First thing I tried," Leia said. "Then their anniversary, all our birthdays, names, Dad's favorite Bible verses and everything I could think of."

Sally paused a long moment and eyed the box.

"Well, worst-case scenario I have some tools back at the garage that will get it open," she said, turning her eyes back to the road. "I spent a lot of time imagining what Dad could be hiding in the attic. Never guessed it could be secret information about a cold-case serial killer. Any idea why he had it?"

"This is where it gets complicated," Leia

said. "Dad told Jay that his best friend from high school—"

"In other words Mom," Sally interjected.

Leia swallowed hard.

"That she went and worked in Toronto for a few months after graduation," Leia said. "There she got involved with Franklin Vamana and saw him kill someone. She was on a trip with him in Niagara Falls at the time and he'd taken her ID and money. She called Dad and he came and rescued her. Franklin threatened to kill Mom and her kid if she told anyone, so she reported it to police anonymously."

"Whoa." Sally blew out a long breath. "Part of me is very surprised—"

"And part of you thinks it all makes sense?" Leia asked. "Yeah, me, too."

"Is it just me or does that sound like Dad's fairy tale about the farmer and the queen?" Sally asked.

"It's not just you," Leia said. "The criminals back at the house were actually looking for Mom, but they knew her by her maiden name. Also, I found a photo album of my baby pictures in the attic." She pressed her lips together and forced herself to say the words. "It looks like I was born in March or April, not June. Which would mean Franklin Vamana is potentially my biological father, not Dad."

For a second Sally didn't move. Then she reached over, took Leia's hand and squeezed it a long moment. "You know that won't change anything between us, right? Or for Rose and Quinn. We love you. Dad loved you. In Dad's eyes and heart you were his daughter. No question. Nothing in the entire world has the power to change that."

Tears filled Leia's eyes and slipped down her cheeks. "Thank you."

Sally pulled her hand away and put both hands on the wheel again.

"Just to be clear, though, you're not getting two birthdays, so you're going to have to choose one," Sally said. Then she blinked. "Did you try your real birthday?"

"No," Leia said. "I never even considered it. I don't know what it would be."

"Keep the day and year the same," Sally said, "and just try a different month."

"Okay."

Could it really be that simple? Leia typed the new date in. There was a click and the box opened. She lifted the lid. There inside sat an old mini cassette player like the kind her dad used to dictate notes into. She held it up for Sally to see and then hit Play.

"Hello, my darlings, it's Mommy." Her mother's voice suddenly filled the truck. Leia reached over, grabbed her sister's arm and squeezed it. "The doctor told me I won't be able to see you grow up. Which makes me a little bit sad, because you're the most important and special things in the world to me and I'd love to be there for you."

Sally sniffled softly.

"So instead, I've written you a bunch of very special stories to remember, about four very strong and brave princesses," Annie's voice went on. "As Daddy knows, the stories all have an important and secret meaning that one day God will help you share to the important people who need to hear it. The first one is about a very busy bee-boy named Jonna Hat and how the princesses rescued him from a big bad guy called Shadow."

Leia stopped the tape recorder. A shiver ran down her limbs.

"They were Mom's stories," Sally said. "Not Dad's. She wrote them, not him. That's why he never came up with any new ones, no matter how many times we asked."

"Mom witnessed the Phantom Killer murder a busboy named Jonathan," Leia said slowly. The shivers grew colder. "In the story, the Shadow hid Jonna Hat under the fountain in a park between a building with a red tin roof and a giant oak tree."

"Each story explained in a lot of detail how the Shadow captured people," Sally said, "and basically provided a map of how the princesses found them. I drew them all out once on the computer when I was a kid."

Hopefully Jay still had the backups of them. If not, she had no doubt her mother had left them enough detail that they could recreate them from her stories.

"Do you think the Phantom Killer, like the Shadow, really hid all his treasures near two waterfalls joined by a river and a rainbow?" Sally added.

"Probably not," Leia said. "But maybe there are more hidden codes and information in the stories. Jay says his mentor knows an amazing tech analyst."

Police may have refused to listen to her mother two decades ago and pursue the case or been bribed by Franklin Vamana to bury it. Leia couldn't imagine how much it had hurt her parents to know a killer had gone free and that no one would take them seriously. How desperate they must have been to protect their baby girl from his revenge. But Leia knew that now the police would have to listen, because she would never drop it and never stop fighting to see the cold cases solved and justice reign. No matter how long it took.

She just prayed Jay would survive and be there to see it.

Headlights appeared in the rearview mirror, growing larger and approaching fast. She glanced at the speedometer. If Sally was already over the speed limit, she shuddered to think just how fast this person was driving. The sound of gunfire sounded behind them. Willie was leaning out of the window, driving with one hand and shooting at them with the other.

Bullets clanged against the back of the truck.

Leia pulled the gun she'd taken off him earlier.

"You okay to drive while I shoot?" Leia asked.

"Absolutely," Sally said. Her hands gripped the steering wheel. "You've got this."

"So do you," Leia said. She rolled the window down again, loosened her seat belt as much as she could.

Sally took one look at her sleeping baby, then hit the gas, pushing the truck faster and faster as it raced into the night.

Leia leaned out of the window and fired.

Her bullets clanged as they hit the hood of the car behind her. Sally swerved sharply. Willie fired again. The back window shattered, sending a spray of safety glass raining down ineffectually over the hood of Mabel's car seat. The baby woke up and started wailing. Leia gritted her teeth and fired again. The car's front tire exploded, sending the vehicle spinning around and around on the slick rain-soaked road. A crunch filled the air as the back corner of the car slammed into a tree. Sally yanked the wheel and spun the truck around in a tight controlled turn until they were facing the car.

Leia leaped from the truck and ran toward the car, holding the gun out with both hands.

"Out of the car now!" she shouted before Willie had even registered what had happened. "Now! Don't even think of reaching for that gun!"

He stumbled from the car and almost fell to his knees, as if dizzy from the impact. She didn't give him a moment to stand. In an instant, Sally was by her side, tying Willie's hands behind his back, gagging his mouth and getting him to lie facedown on the ground, while Leia stood guard over him.

Sally patted him down quickly, practically shouting with victory as she found a cell phone. She held it to his face to unlock the screen with facial recognition.

"We've got a cell phone signal!" Sally's face beamed with joy while determination shone in her eyes. "Time to call 9-1-1, get them out there and end this whole thing."

Leia glanced at the car. The motor was still running, and the keys dangled from the ignition.

"To answer your question," Sally said before Leia even could ask it, "it'll take me less than five minutes to verify the car's still safe to drive and change the tire if there's a spare, if you'll watch over Willie here and keep an ear out for Mabel."

Leia pressed her lips together. "Will you be okay if I left you?"

"Absolutely," Sally said. "Willie's not going anywhere, so I can drive off with Mabel in the truck at the first sign of trouble and, most importantly, I'll be on the phone with 9-1-1 the whole time. Just start the call now, pass the phone to me when you leave and make sure I've got a gun."

"Got it." Leia's chin rose. "Thanks."

Fresh determination filled her core as she took in a deep breath. She was going back to the farmhouse to rescue Jay.

Just please still be alive.

TWELVE

Pain filled Jay's shoulders as he sat on a wooden chair in the living room of the Dukes farmhouse with both hands tied tightly behind his back. He could hear the ticking of the grandfather clock mingling with the light patter of rain outside but had no idea how long he'd been at the criminals' mercy. From what he could tell, they were down to just two armed men now. Dunlop was dead; Willie had gone after Sally and Leia, and Ben had apparently disappeared into the night after escaping the burning barn.

At first Stan and Ross had seemed happy just to yell abuse at him a bit, tie him up tightly and threaten terrible things. Then they headed off to keep searching the house, considering him to be nothing but an unfortunate nuisance unrelated to whatever they were looking for, leaving him to worry for Leia's safety and think about the fact his evidence wall had been swallowed up in the barn fire, which mercifully the rain had then turned to smoldering ashes before it could spread.

Now the pounding of footsteps on the floorboards told him they were back. For a moment he let his eyes close in prayer, asking God for courage and help as he battled the fear in his chest. He looked up to see two of the men whose faces had just been mug shots on the evidence wall now standing over him. Between them they'd been accused of seven murders, along with countless violent assaults and extortion threats. He asked God to bring these men and all those who'd been on the wall to justice, even if he didn't live to see it.

Just stay alive, Jay. The words of his mentor, Jess Stone, filled his mind. *When you're faced with the worst, do your job, hold on to faith and stay alive. Your brothers and sisters in blue are always coming for you.*

But how could they if they didn't even know he was in trouble?

"Give me one good reason why I shouldn't break your limbs and shoot you right now," Stan said.

"I know where Ann-Margret Herber is," Jay said.

His answer was blunt, direct, honest and definitely not what the criminals were expecting based on how wide their eyes went. Stan's hand flew across Jay's face in a slap, snapping his back.

"Where is she?" he shouted.

"Hey!" Jay shouted. "There's no need for all that! I'm cooperating!"

Stan stepped back like he was shocked by Jay's defiance. Ross chuckled. It was a threatening sound.

"Then where is she?" Stan shouted.

"She'd dead," Jay said honestly.

Ross's derisive laughter grew louder.

"He don't know nothing!" Ross said. He pulled his gun and pressed the barrel right between Jay's eyes. "He's just some guy that was hired to work around the place. We got no reason to keep him alive."

For the first time in his life, Jay felt the overwhelming urge to blow his cover well up inside him. Sure, he'd been warned to expect it. It was a trial every undercover officer faced at some point in their career. But he hadn't been prepared for just how urgently the need to stay alive would hit him and how desperately he needed to see

Leia's face again and know that she was okay, even as his logical brain shouted that telling these thugs he was a cop would do nothing to make his death less inevitable or painful.

Something moved in the shadows to his right. He glanced over to see Moses sitting behind a large black duffel bag that lay on the floor by the couch. It wasn't exactly the kind of backup that Jay would've wanted, but somehow it helped to know he wasn't alone. The cat disappeared into the shadows. Jay thought about how Walter's memory had continued to guide Leia long after he was gone. Suddenly, John 8:32 crossed his mind the way Leia had recalled the verses that Walter had taught her. But this verse hadn't come from Walter. It had been one of Jay's own father's favorite verses and one he'd lived his life by.

And ye shall know the truth, and the truth shall make you free.

Truth was, Leia, Sally and Mabel were safe; they'd found the hidden box in the attic, and one way or another the wheels of justice had already started turning even if he never lived to see how the story ended.

"Listen up," Jay said. "You're right, I was hired to be a farmhand here, which means I talked to people, listened to what they said and know things. I'm going to tell you the honest truth. And if you hadn't been foolish enough to take out the cell tower you might even have been able to verify every single thing I tell you on the internet. So pay attention and take this message back to your boss, Franklin Vamana. About thirty-five years ago, Ann-Margret got married and changed her name to Annie Dukes. There'll be government records to back that up, along with the fact that she died a few years later. If she did leave anything behind about Franklin, it's long gone now. So, all this tearing up the house and threatening people is getting you nowhere."

Ross's laughter began to peter out like the way a man chuckled nervously when he suddenly lost confidence that he was on the right side of a joke. Stan's hand flew across Jay's face in another backhanded slap. But this time, instead of pain, all Jay felt was righteous anger. These men might be monsters but at their core they were nothing but bullies and he'd dealt with bullies.

"What's even the point of all this?" Jay yelled. "Because it makes no sense to me. What can your boss possibly think is so important that he'd send you all here in the middle of the night to terrorize people. Do you even know?"

A car engine rumbled outside. Tires screeched as it came to a stop. But the criminals holding him were done with questions and answers. In a swift and brutal motion, Stan shoved the chair, sending Jay flying backward to the ground. His head cracked back against the floor. Agony shot through his limbs. Stan stepped his foot onto Jay's throat.

"Here's what's going to happen," Stan said. "I'm going to ask the questions, but you're not going to speak unless directed. If I don't like the answers I'm going to hurt you. Got it?"

"No, you're not!" Leia's voice filled the air, determined and strong, sending shivers through Jay's core. "You're going to let him go. Right now!"

What was she doing? Lord, keep her safe.

Stunned silence fell thick through the room. Jay glanced past Stan and saw Leia towering over him as she stood firm in the middle of her family living room. She wasn't holding a gun or any weapon in her hands, and yet she was swathed in some invisible cloak of confidence and courage that took his breath away.

"This is my family home," she said, "and you're not welcome here. Get out while you can."

Stan snorted. "You have any idea what I'm going to do to you?" he snarled. "Who do you think you are to stand up to me?"

"I'm the eldest sister in this family," she said. "That's what matters most to me. But for you? I'm the biological daughter of Franklin Vamana. That means the one man you're probably most afraid of has every reason to be afraid of me. If you kill me, my sisters will go to the police and the press, with photos and evidence claiming Franklin Vamana ordered his own child killed. They'll fight in the courts for a DNA test proving it. He'll be ruined. His family's businesses will be destroyed. Whatever he's hoping to accomplish here will be nothing. Now. Let. Jay. Go."

A pregnant pause filled the living room. Then the criminals turned their weapons on her.

"You're coming with us and we're taking you to the boss," Stan said. "Now. And if you're lying, we'll kill you."

"I will come with you and cooperate," Leia said. "But only if you let Jay go."

"No!" Jay shouted. His heart was pounding so hard he thought his rib cage might shatter. His bound hands, now pinned by the weight of his body, struggled against the chair. "No, Leia, you can't let them take you!"

Leia's eyes met his and he could see his own anguish mirrored there. She started across the floor toward him. Immediately Ross stepped in front of her, weapon raised, but she pushed past him like he wasn't even there.

She crouched down beside Jay, leaned over and lightly placed her lips against his cheek.

"Sally's on the phone with 9-1-1," she whispered. "Help is on the way. Don't worry, this is just a stalling tactic to keep you alive until then. Cops will block the roads, backup will arrive and it'll all be okay. They won't dare hurt me and you'll be two steps behind."

"I'll find you," Jay whispered.

"I know," Leia said. She bent down and brushed a quick kiss across his lips. He heard the faint sound of wood snapping and realized she'd purposely cracked one of the spindles on the back of the chair.

"Hurry up!" Stan bellowed.

Stan grabbed Leia by the arm and yanked

her to her feet. Ross picked up a heavy bag of weapons off the ground and slung it over his shoulder. Jay watched as they marched her out through the kitchen, feeling something tear in his chest as if they were pulling out a piece of him as they went. He gritted his teeth so hard his jaw ached. He struggled against his bonds, twisting his body against the broken spindle and fighting his own exhausted limbs' desire to pause. Slowly, bit by bit, he felt the wood crack under his weight until finally he was able to wrench his hands free, enough to roll onto his side and push himself up. He stumbled to his feet and ran into the kitchen, dragging behind him a piece of the chair still connected to his bound hands.

The kitchen was empty, and the back door lay open. Where had they taken Leia? He found the knife block, felt around behind with his hands for a steak knife and used it to hack his hands from the wood. Finally, his hands were free and he could move again.

Sirens filled the air, feet pounded, voices filled the air and, within an instant, police stormed the farmhouse on all sides. Instinctively, his hands rose above his head even while his heart leaped to see the wave of figures in flak jackets, bulletproof vests and helmets.

Then he saw the diminutive form of his mentor, Jess, striding through the group toward him. The detective's long blond hair was tied back in a smart bun. The armed officers parted for her like the proverbial sea, despite the fact she barely came up to their shoulders.

"Good to see you," he said. "They took Leia."

"Where?" Jess asked.

"I'm not sure exactly," he said. "They went out the back. I'm positive they're taking her to Franklin Vamana in Toronto."

"How big's their head start?" she asked.

"Maybe ten minutes," he said. "Probably even less."

"Come on," Jess said. She gave a signal and within moments a weapon was handed to him by an officer to his right. They ran out the back door, flanked by armed and uniformed officers on both sides. An officer shone his flashlight over the trees. A path of footprints and broken branches lay before them. "This way."

Jay pelted up the path, feeling the strength of his fellow officers and mentor around him like a wave. The criminals were outnumbered and outgunned. He would rescue Leia, this would all be over and she'd be safe. The trees broke and a steep grass hill lay ahead, with the demolished cell tower at the top. Jay pressed himself onward as they ran up the hill.

A roar overtook the air ahead of him, so deep and loud it sounded like a wall of thunder rising straight up from the top of the hill. Fierce wind whipped against his body, and a light shone down on him. He looked up to see a helicopter rising into the sky, climbing higher and higher by the moment. And he knew with every beat of his pain-filled heart that Leia was on it.

He dropped to his knees on the wet grass, blocking out the voices of the officers around him.

Leia had been kidnapped, snatched away from him, and she was gone.

Leia's desperate eyes stared down at the treetops as Jay's form disappeared from sight. For a fleeting moment she'd seen him there, running through the trees after her, flanked by people with flashlights coming for her. And everything in her heart had leaped with the hope that he would make it. Instead, she'd been forced to watch helplessly as the helicopter rose, leaving him behind.

Finally, even the ground below disappeared into the darkness.

She leaned back against the seat, strapped in tightly by the shoulder harness seat belt. The sound of the rotors was so deafening that it seemed to be coming from every direction at once and radiating through her body. Both Ross, who was piloting the helicopter, and Stan, who was in the back pointing a weapon at her, were wearing headsets, which meant they could communicate with each other. But without one, she could barely make out a word they were saying, lost as they were in the noise and vibrations surrounding her.

"Ack!" Suddenly Stan leaped from his seat as if Ross's bag, which lay on the floor, had bitten him. "There's something in here!"

The helicopter swung wildly to the right as Ross spun around and looked back over his shoulder. Stan lurched and stumbled, falling against the side of the helicopter. Leia grabbed her seat belt harness tightly. As she watched, Moses leaped from the bag; his fur was standing on end and his eyes were wild. The cat shot across the helicopter and into Leia's lap. She wrapped her arms around his frightened form.

"It's the cat!" Stan hollered, and Leia wasn't sure if he'd yelled so loudly that she'd actually heard the words or had just read his lips. He grabbed a handle above the door with one wildly shaking hand and with the other aimed his gun at the cat on her lap.

"Stop!" Ross yelled back over his shoulder, and again she wasn't sure if she'd actually heard him. "Sit down!"

"Let go of the cat!" Stan shouted at Leia. The gun still waved in front of her.

"Sit down!" Leia screamed, not even knowing if Stan could hear her. "You're not shooting a cat in a helicopter!"

Did he even realize how idiotically impossible trying to shoot anything was in a helicopter? Let alone a small animal?

She prayed hard and cradled the cat to her chest, staring the criminal down until finally the helicopter righted and Stan sat back down and, this time, fastened his seat belt. A tense stalemate filled the helicopter and after a while Moses's fur relaxed. She closed her eyes and felt the cat's rumbling purr through her fingertips.

Jay's face filled her mind. She remembered the way his smile quirked when he thought she was saying something funny, and the dark intensity in his eyes when they'd kissed. But even more, she thought about the way he cared about those in need and how relentless he was in pursuing the things that mattered to him.

Jay had promised that he would find her and she knew that he would.

Everything would somehow be okay. These criminals were taking her to meet her biological father, Franklin Vamana, and that was probably at his hotel and office in Toronto. Police would raid it and find her. She had to have faith.

From the end of the earth will I cry unto Thee, when my heart is overwhelmed: lead me to the rock that is higher than I.

She drifted in and out of consciousness and didn't even realize she'd fallen asleep until she felt the helicopter suddenly begin to drop beneath her. She looked out the window but saw nothing but city lights shining against the predawn black.

Stan undid his seat belt and leaned over toward her. There was a strip of cloth in his hands. He blindfolded her firmly and she didn't fight it, knowing she had nothing to gain by struggling or trying to make a break for it while they were still in the air.

The helicopter landed with a jolt that seemed to shake through her; the cat disappeared from her lap and she felt the rush of cold air as a door opened. The rotors began to slow, and he felt Stan grab her arm and pull her to her feet. His other hand pushed her head down for a moment as they climbed through the low doorway and out into the wind. She was walked across the tarmac, flanked by people on both sides, and something about the air filling her lungs told her she was on the roof of a skyscraper. As the rumble of the helicopter began to dissipate, she was aware of another deep rushing sound she couldn't place.

She was propelled off the roof, through a door, down a flight of steps, along a hallway and finally down another flight of steps. Then she was tugged to a stop.

"Hold her still," an unfamiliar male voice said.

Suddenly her right arm was being practically yanked out of its socket as a rough pair of hands stretched it out to its full extension. There was a sharp jab and she felt a needle pierce her skin on the inside of her elbow. Leia yelped. It felt like they were drawing blood. The moment seemed endless as she waited for the needle to be withdrawn.

A door opened, she was lead inside and then she heard that door shut behind her.

The world fell silent again, except for the strange rushing sound she couldn't place. She took off her blindfold and found herself alone in a hotel room. A small prick of blood on her inner arm remained from where someone had taken a blood sample. Looked like they'd decided to run a DNA test.

At first glance, the hotel room was small but lavish. But as she investigated it further, she discovered it had been conscientiously stripped of every single thing that could be used as a weapon; it was like a high-end prison cell. There was a bed with nothing but a thick down duvet on it, and a chunky desk, which was bolted to the floor. Heavy blinds were drawn across the window without curtains. Every drawer was empty as was the minifridge, and the only towels in the bathroom were small, fluffy hand towels. An array of tiny samples of Indigo Iris cosmetics, hair and beauty products sat artfully beside the sink.

The hotel door clicked open again and she glanced through a crack in the open door to see two young and well-dressed men in sharp suits and ties stepping into the room, and Stan behind them with his weapon drawn. One of the men set a paper bowl of fresh fruit, paper plates of cheese and meat and a plastic cup of water on the desk. The other laid a pair of soft pink yoga pants, T-shirt, sweatshirt, socks and slippers on the bed. Then they left without a word.

It was like they'd been planning on her trying to escape or fight her way out and had been determined to rob her of every possible weapon. Did that mean she should freshen up and eat something? When was she meeting Franklin Vamana? How long until Jay found her?

And where was that rushing noise coming from?

She crossed to the window, opened the blinds, looked out and gasped. The towering waters of Niagara Falls poured into its basin below her, sending a plume of mist soaring upward as the waterfall roared.

She wasn't in Franklin Vamana's building. She was nowhere near Toronto.

Jay had no idea how to find her. She was on her own.

THIRTEEN

The predawn raid by the police on the Vamana Enterprises building on Lakeshore Boulevard in Toronto moved like a well-oiled machine. Over thirty Ontario and Toronto police officers were already in tactical position around the building, waiting for the moment when the warrant arrived authorizing their mission. Then they'd swarmed the forty-two-story building, securing both exits and staff, as Jess strode to the security desk and announced, "We have a warrant to search this facility for Miss Leia Dukes and question Mr. Franklin Vamana in relation to her kidnapping."

It had been barely more than an hour since Jay had watched helplessly as Leia had been kidnapped and whisked away by helicopter. Jay was endlessly thankful that Jess had been put in charge of the operation, instead of any number of other officers it could've been. Her authority and command of the scene was unquestionable, and she'd been quick to authorize Jay to take part while still maintaining his cover. Now, he was dressed in the smart, blue-black uniform of a Toronto beat cop, complete with the deep-brimmed hat, with its wide red band, pulled low over his eyes and hiding half his face. The lower part of his face was disguised with a trim and surprisingly realistic-looking beard. It reminded him of his father.

Jay followed closely behind the senior officer as a startled security guard led Jess and a small phalanx of officers up the elevator to Franklin's apartment. She knocked sharply, announced they were police and then burst in.

Franklin Vamana, the billionaire CEO of an entertainment industry and presumed cold-case serial killer, was sitting alone in a large armchair, while both a shocked but tired-looking male nurse and a grumpy security guard stood beside him. His gray hair was meticulously groomed, and his housecoat was scarlet.

Jess announced herself and read off the list of charges.

Franklin snorted. "I've never heard of

Leia Dukes, but feel free to search my building. You won't find her. As for the men who allegedly raided her farmhouse and abducted her, I haven't had any dealings with them for years."

His smile was smug, bordering on a smirk, and radiated a confidence that worried Jay.

Jay waited, behind Jess, in a small group of officers while she peppered Franklin with questions he refused to answer about Leia, her mother, the fact he was allegedly Leia's father and the Phantom Killer. Her walkietalkie crackled occasionally with officers announcing their designated search area was clear, until finally the entire building was swept.

With each moment that passed, doubt dripped into Jay's core until it pooled in a puddle of despair. If Leia wasn't there, where was she?

Help me, Lord! She's in danger and I was wrong.

"Let me save you some trouble," Franklin said. "If I allegedly had a daughter, kidnapping her and bringing her here would be the furthest thing from my mind. I have no children, because I want none. If a person did claim to be my child, I'd make myself very clear that they were not, and to never mention it again."

"There are such things as paternity tests," Jess snapped back.

"No person who knows me would be foolish enough to take one," Franklin said. Then Franklin's smirk hardened angrily into a sneer. "I want you to know that I will destroy your life for this, Detective Jessica Stone."

He drew out her title and full name to every syllable for emphasis.

"Maybe I will sue you in the courts for harassment," he went on. "Or I'll talk to the good friends I know within the police and make sure you're investigated for misconduct, and your entire career will be tanked. Maybe the tabloids will start trailing your family and digging up every possible skeleton of your husband's past, including planting a few. Or strange men will start watching your children in the playground—you won't know why and you'll never quite feel safe."

He chuckled as if the well-coiffed man in his smart red dressing gown relished the thought. Tension built up Jay's spine like a tight coil ready to spring. He'd always known, if not suspected, that threats like this were how Franklin had gotten away with nobody investigating his crimes and how the information Annie had provided to the police thirty-five years ago got buried. But witnessing it in person was an entirely different thing. It shook him.

But Jess just nodded professionally. "We'll be in touch."

She turned, stepped out into the hallway and signaled for Jay to join her, and the other cops to stay. She sent a quick text and then spoke to Jay.

"Don't worry," she said. "We'll find Leia. I promise. And then we'll get the proof to take him down. We can't arrest him yet until we build that case and lock it down. But he won't get away with this."

"Thank you," Jay said. He knew it was one thing to know in his heart that Franklin Vamana was a serial killer and quite another to hammer down the proof beyond a reasonable doubt needed to prove it in court. He blew out a long breath. "Are you okay? He sounded pretty vicious."

"Oh, yeah." Jess rolled her eyes. "He's not the first man to threaten me and I'm sure he won't be the last. Now, just give me a second to regroup and we'll figure out our next move."

Jay closed his eyes and prayed. *Lord, help us and keep Leia save.*

"Hello!" Franklin's voice rose, summoning them from the other room as if they were waitstaff. "Is that Jayce? Hey, Jayce, come talk to me."

A sudden, palpable fear, such as he'd never experienced before, washed over Jay like a wave, freezing the blood in his veins, as he heard the serial killer call his birth name.

"Breathe," Jess said, "and that's an order from a superior officer. Don't let him provoke you."

"It's Jayce Starling, right?" Franklin's voice had a teasing and menacing lilt. "It's been a very long time, but I'm pretty good at faces. You were named after your father, right? Come talk to me, little Jayce, about your daddy."

He wondered if his face was as pale as it felt. *Maintain your cover. Don't let this monster steal that from you.*

"It's amazing what a man will tell you when he knows he's about to die," Franklin taunted. "Hypothetically, of course. He might say, 'Please, I've got a wife. I've got a son. He's just a little boy. You can kill me but don't kill my boy!'"

Jay's fists clenched and unclenched at his sides.

"Don't react," Jess said. "He's just guessing at your identity, that's all. Some people happen to be exceptionally good at remembering and identifying faces. You've met plenty of them in law enforcement."

"But he's confessing to killing my father..."

"I know," Jess said. "But he's too smart to say anything that will hold up in court. Don't let him provoke you into doing something you'll regret." Then his superior officer turned back toward Franklin. "If you have anything to say to my officers you can say it to me."

Jay closed his eyes so tightly he practically clenched them. Leia's beautiful face filled his mind, filling him with strength. He would find her and rescue her. As much as he loved his father, who'd fueled Jay's passion to take down the Phantom Killer, his past was behind him. Whatever happened next with Leia was the future.

Lord, help me be strong.

A text pinged from somewhere behind him. Then Jess swiftly pulled him aside.

"So how do you feel about total longshots?" she asked.

"That sometimes they're the only shot we've got," Jay said. "Why? How out of the box are we talking?"

"Very," Jess said. "I'm almost embarrassed to bring it up. As you know, I have a good friend, Seth, who's a tech genius. I asked him to see if there was anything interesting popping up on social media or public domain sites about any Vamana properties. Nothing needing a warrant, just whatever he could glean, and fast. I told him to inform me of anything weird. Anything at all. No matter how seemingly irrelevant to this case."

Considering this case that sounded like a good way to go about it.

"And he found something?" Jay asked.

"Nothing relevant, but yes," she said. "Only in Niagara Falls."

A jolt of electricity brushed Jay's spine. Leia's mother Annie had been in Niagara Falls with Franklin when Walter had driven through the night to save her.

Jess held the phone and Jay looked down at a blurry picture of a small brown, white and black tabby.

"Apparently there's a stray cat prowling one of Vamana's five-star casino buildings in Niagara Falls," she said. "Does that mean anything to you?"

* * *

Leia had no idea how long she'd been held captive in the lavish hotel room. There was no clock in the room or even a television, let alone a phone. She'd scoured the room in vain for anything that could be used as a weapon, and after checking the food thoroughly for any potential tampering, she decided it was important to take the risk and eat. Her father had always taught her that food and sleep were two of the most important things someone needed before a fight, so she rolled herself up in the duvet and catnapped, too.

When she'd awoken, she freshened up, washed her face, braided her hair and put together a hybrid outfit out of her own clothes and the ones they'd offered her. She ignored the makeup, except for grabbing the one tiny perfume sample she figured might briefly sting an attacker's eyes and buy her a moment in a pinch.

Then there was nothing left to do but pray, pace and wait for battle.

Finally, the door opened, and she found herself stretching to full height as she turned to face it. There stood Stan and Ross, two of the men who'd kidnapped her in her own farmhouse the night before, still holding weapons at her. By the look of things, they were still in the same dirty clothes they'd been wearing all night.

"Turn around," Stan said. "I'm going to blindfold you."

There was less of a confident snarl in his voice than she was used to and more of a resigned, simmering anger. Not that she was about to battle two heavily armed men twice her size and survive. *Lord, show me my moment. Tell me when to act.*

She turned her back and let him blindfold her eyes, contorting her facial muscles as soon as her face was out of his sight to ensure the cloth would be as loose as possible. Then she turned back and let them march her down the hallway yet again.

Fear battled against faith in her heart. Where was Jay? Had she been wrong? Had she just walked into the lion's den like the biblical story of Daniel? If so, would God save her?

A door opened in front of her with a sweeping sound that told her two opposing doors were swinging back like some kind of grand entrance.

"Leave us." The voice was female, crisp and assured.

The double door slammed behind her. The floor creaked.

"My my, you are pretty," the voice said. Leia felt the figure walking around her in a circle like a sculpture being evaluated. "You can take off the blindfold."

Leia did so and looked up to see Esther Vamana standing in front of her. She blinked. What was this?

"Where's Franklin?" she asked.

"Not here," Esther said, as if the question was completely inconsequential.

Despite the early hour, the older woman was impeccably dressed with exquisitely applied makeup, a matching pearl pendant and earrings and a long and sweeping turquois jacket that seemed to perfectly complement her stylishly short silver hair. Leia looked past her and around the room. It was an expansive and lush office, with a huge magnificent desk, two couches and several large and ornate pieces of modern art, which wouldn't make half-bad defensive weapons if she could lift them. Huge floor-to-ceiling windows behind her turned the entire wall into a sheet of glass, which gave a panoramic view of Niagara Falls at the crack of dawn, awash in gentle hues of pink and blue.

Then she watched as an object slowly rose

into view on two thin cables she hadn't even noticed at first glance. The top of a hat appeared and then she saw the window washer. He was suspended outside the building dozens of stories off the ground, in a long and thin metal cage. He was tall, and dressed in a workman's jumpsuit that matched the safety harness that clipped him to the railing. He had a long and full bushy beard like a lumberjack and the rest of his face was buried in a blue baseball hat.

Then his gaze rose to meet Leia's and joy exploded like fireworks through her heart.

It was Jay! He'd found her, he'd come for her, and now the man who was afraid of heights was suspended several stories above the falls, alone. Jay raised his squeegee and started soaping the window.

"Your eyes really are purple," Esther said. Her manicured hand lightly clasped Leia's chin, turning her face back toward her. "My mother had purple eyes, too, you know. Indigo irises, in fact. I'm told it's a rare genetic mutation that's passed down. Sadly, it missed a generation with my brother and me."

"Why did you send all those goons to my family farmhouse last night?" Leia demanded. "Why did they ransack the place and kidnap me?"

Esther blinked and stepped back, shocked, as if one of the pieces of art in her office collection had spoken to her.

"Does it really matter now?" she asked. "I was looking for something to use to pressure my sick brother into signing his shares over to me and giving me a controlling interest of the company before he rallied and recovered. I got a tip through a police contact that someone had been running around telling stories to a junior officer about my brother and an unknown woman, who I realized had to be Ann-Margret Herber. So I got the name of his source and sent some people I knew to the late man's farm to see if there was anything to it. I had no idea your mother was dead or that you existed. We hadn't exactly kept tabs on her after we quashed the stories she tried to sell to the police. I believe my father tried to find her and failed."

Leia glanced at Jay's strong form washing the windows outside. And even though she'd only seen his face for a fleeting moment, disguised by the hat and beard and even couldn't see it now, just knowing he was there filled her with confidence. Esther glanced around, and Leia held her breath, but then the glamorous older woman turned back as if the sight of a figure soaping the window outside was nothing more than scenery. Leia suspected she went through life often dismissing seemingly irrelevant people that way.

"Did you know that one of the men you sent was murdered by another one?" Leia demanded. "Or that another one, a young father, was trapped in a barn fire and nearly died?"

"And a third was arrested," Esther said, like they were discussing the path of ants on a driveway, "and it will take a lot of money and hassle to shut him up. Yes, I know. You're completely missing the bigger picture."

A gust of wind shook the metal platform outside the window. Leia watched helplessly as Jay gripped the edges of the railing for a moment. His fake beard flapped in the wind so hard that for a moment she was afraid it was about to blow off. Then the gust died down and Jay returned to cleaning. Her heart ached. What was even the plan? How was she going to escape this?

Jay was so very close and yet still so far away.

Esther took a step back and leaned against the desk.

"I have good news," Esther said, as if about to bestow a gift beyond measure on her. "The blood tests came back positive. You're indeed my brother's daughter and my niece. Franklin has been waiting for months on the transplant list and we've been helpless to procure him one. His blood type is rare, and the official organ list is long. Thanks to some police investigation, the private market for organ sales is simply impossible to access in Canada right now."

In other words, black market organs.

"So, you kidnapped me to force me to help your brother stay alive?" Leia said, the full horror of the situation slowly dawning on her.

"Not necessarily," Esther said. "Even if you come forward publicly as a potential donor, it puts my brother in my debt even if it never goes through. In exchange for extremely good financial compensation, of course, and that's just for starters. I'm willing to pay your law school tuition in full at the university of your choice, provide you with a healthy living allowance and an apartment in downtown Toronto and cancel your debts. As for your three sisters, all of them have considerable debts, do they not? Consider them paid, along with each of them receiving a very generous handout to enable them to live the lives of their dreams."

Leia felt her mouth open. She knew about her sisters?

"I was doing my homework while you were resting," Esther said, as if reading the unspoken question on her lips. "Your family has struggled considerably financially. I'm offering to take care of all of that and give you a fresh start at life. I also hear you're involved with some farmhand? If you wish, I can arrange for him to be taken care of, as well. I'm not promising you can have a public relationship, but if it matters to you, something private can be arranged."

Did this mean Jay's cover hadn't been blown and they still had no idea the farmhand was an undercover cop?

Leia met Jay's wide eyes over Esther's shoulders. He could hear them somehow. No doubt it had been nearly impossible to get a recording device actually inside the room. Was there a high-powered microphone on his window-washing rig? Perhaps police were even recording the conversation.

"In exchange for a transplant," Leia said.

"No," Esther said. "For a good story! The

press is going to eat up the idea of a long-lost daughter making a national appeal for my brother and stepping up to care for him. You'll be a media darling. You work for the less fortunate and you're undeniably beautiful. Your story will be compelling, and everyone wins. Perhaps his health will improve, and he won't even need anything more. No promises, but it's possible."

"As long as you get control of his company," Leia supplied, "and can use my existence to blackmail him."

"Yes," Esther said, "and every bit of rumor, allegation or evidence to my brother's unfortunate past is permanently erased and refuted."

"So, you want me to cover up the fact your brother is a serial killer," Leia said, "and trade my happiness at the thought of justice for his victims and peace for their families…for money."

Esther's lips curled in a sneer and suddenly no amount of makeup or coiffing could hide the ugliness in her face.

"You don't get it," Esther said. "You have no power here. Just because I'm offering you a once-in-a-lifetime opportunity to transform your life doesn't mean I won't just take what I want if the answer is no."

But again Leia glanced past her to the glorious world outside and the strong form of the man she admired most in the world. As she watched, he wrote J832 in the suds before wiping it clean. John 8:32. *Ye shall know the truth, and the truth shall make you free.*

Leia felt her chin rise. "The answer is no."

Esther's blue eyes grew and her perfectly painted mouth set in a thin line. She pressed a button on her desk and the double doors swung open again. Stan and Ross strode into the room.

"Take her," Esther said. "Restrain her and sedate her."

The criminals came toward her. There was a syringe in Stan's hand. Instinctively Leia backed up toward the window.

"It's a pity," Esther said. "I would've enjoyed dressing you up and managing your image. It could've been big for the company. But a sleeping beauty in a medically induced coma is more practical, I suppose."

Fear rose up Leia's spine. She prayed that Jay saw what was happening.

The explosion of a high-powered weapon sounded behind her; the floor to-ceiling window exploded, and a sudden wind rushed in as glass cascaded through the room like a wave.

"Leia!" Jay shouted. "Come on!"

She turned and ran across the floor toward the shattered remains of the window and the open sky beyond. Jay opened his arms for her. The window-washing platform began to drop.

She leaped over the ledge.

FOURTEEN

Jay opened his arms, and she tumbled into them and felt him clutch her to his chest as the window-washing platform slid back down the side of the building. She held him tightly and he held her just as fiercely as a wind rushed past them and the platform dropped at a swift but controlled pace. Bullets echoed from the floors high above them as criminals tried futilely to fire after them, only to give up quickly as they apparently realized there was no safe way to lean out the gaping hole Jay's weapon had left behind, let alone hit the moving target in the wind.

She prayed and thanked God for rescue and that Jay was safe.

"Told you I'd find you," he called, raising his voice against the rushing sound of the falls below as the wind whipped around them. He stepped back just enough to help her slide into a safety harness and clip her in. Then went back to embracing her. "Are you okay?"

"Yes!" she practically shouted back. "I'm fine. But what about you? We're forty stories off the ground."

"Don't remind me," he said, and chuckled. "And before you ask—nope, I'm not getting used to it."

"What about the beard?" she yelled.

"I'm not keeping that, either!" he said.

She leaned against the warmth of his core, and despite the height, she was feeling secure in a way she couldn't put into words.

"How did you even find me?" she asked. "I thought you'd assume they'd taken me to Franklin's offices in Toronto."

"I did!" he said. "But Moses tipped me off you were here."

She laughed. "How?"

Jay reached around her and pressed a button, and the window-washing platform started to slow the pace of its descent.

"We initialized a full-scale predawn raid on Franklin's offices in Toronto," Jay said. "He claimed to have nothing to do with your kidnapping. Police made a full search of the building and of course didn't find any trace of you. The mentor I mentioned, Detective

Jess Stone, is in charge of the operation and she texted her tech friend, Seth, to see if he could spot anything on camera feeds at other Vamana properties. Anything at all, no matter how weird or irrelevant. It was a total long shot. But sure enough he found something online about a random brown, white and black tabby cat wandering around a building in Niagara Falls. And then I remembered that your dad had rescued your mom from Niagara, not Toronto."

Her mind boggled.

"Moses hitched a ride on the helicopter in one of the criminals' bags," she said. "He's notorious for falling asleep in bags."

And where was the cat now? she wondered. Had he found a new home, or kept roaming or somehow come back?

She looked up and estimated that Jay had already put ten stories' distance between himself and the shattered window above. She glanced nervously at the building windows as they moved past her, but saw only her own reflection and the sky above mirrored back.

"What's to stop criminals from figuring out what floor we're about to pass next and just shooting us through the window?" she asked.

"Police," Jay said, dropping his voice back to speaking level now that the wind in their ears had dissipated some. He turned to face her again and her heart swelled as she traced the lines of his face. "Joint provincial and local police initiatives are moving in to lock down the building as we speak. They'd just been awaiting my confirmation that you were on the premises and where you were located."

"So, you went in undercover," she said.

"I did," he said, "and I hated every moment up off the ground."

She laughed.

"But it was worth it," he said. One arm slid tight around her waist, and the other slid to her face. He cupped her cheek in his hand. "Knowing you were okay and laying eyes on you was worth everything to me."

"Well, I've got to say I'm not a fan of this beard," she teased.

"Consider it gone the moment I'm not at risk of being identified," he said. He glanced down and she followed his gaze. At least twenty police vehicles had surrounded the building now, including a gawking crowd and news vans. Jay pushed the button again and the platform stopped halfway down the side of the building.

Something warm and comforting pooled in his eyes. A voice in the back of her mind reminded her that she couldn't just let herself keep falling into this man's arms when she was scared. Yes, he'd found her when she was in danger and scaled the side of a building to keep her safe. But that didn't mean that he was ready to be in a relationship with her. Or that she could let herself love him.

And yet somehow her hands slid up into his hair and then his lips found hers. He kissed her and she kissed him back, for one brief moment letting herself feel complete in his arms. Then he pulled away, and she tucked her head into his shoulder and shivered against him.

"You cold?" he asked.

"Just scared mostly," she admitted. It was like somehow she'd managed to hold it together for the entire ordeal, from the first moment she'd been grabbed when she stepped through her front door, through being chased, kidnapped, threatened, taken captive and then finally when she found herself face-to-face with an unexpected and surprising evil. And now that she was safe, the full weight of what she'd been through was finally hitting her at once. "I'm okay, but this night has been the scariest of my life."

"Mine, too," Jay said.

He hugged her for one long moment. Then he let her go, turned and looked out at where the sun rose slowly over the falls. His hands gripped the railing.

"But it's all over now," he added. "Police secured your family farm and made sure Sally and the baby were okay. Local police in the jurisdictions where Quinn and Rose live are checking up on them, and Sally has already talked with them both. Willie was arrested by the side of the road. Sally still had him at gunpoint when police arrived. The coroner has taken away Dunlop. Police will make sure any remaining family are contacted, and if no one claims his body, then he'll be given a dignified burial. No one's seen Ben ever since he escaped the burning barn back at the farm. But both Stan and Ross will leave this building in handcuffs, as will Esther Vamana. I also recorded every word Esther said with a high-powered microphone and relayed it back to police on the ground. We have all the evidence we need. But I expect you'll be questioned by my colleague Jess, who's now heading the operation, and also be asked to testify when it goes to trial."

"So, this means your cover was never blown?" she said. "You succeeded in staying undercover this entire time."

"I did," he said. "I came very close to giving it up at one point. Franklin recognized me as my father's son and started taunting me. For a second I didn't think I was going to keep it together."

"I can only imagine," she said. "That must've been hard."

"It was," he said. "But I stayed strong, held my tongue and didn't crack."

"Well, you've always been good at controlling your feelings," she said slowly.

While she'd just let her own emotions run roughshod over her mind yet again.

Lord, as much as I care about this man, I need to change. It's time I respect myself enough to save my heart for someone who wants a life with me.

He didn't look at her. Instead, his gaze searched the stunning waterfall vista below. She stood beside him and did likewise. Their arms bumped. And she knew this moment together, suspended on a rickety metal platform off the edge of a skyscraper, was nothing more than another sweet and stolen moment between them. Nothing more. They were just sharing one final goodbye in a long and painful string of goodbyes they'd had so far.

Help me, Lord. Make me strong enough to say goodbye to this man again.

Jay took a deep breath, as if trying to delay his next sentence as long as possible. So she said it for them.

"The fact your cover wasn't blown means nothing changes for you, right?" she said. "You're going to head out from here into your undercover work, fulfill your dreams and take down every single face on that board."

Without a wife and without a family.

Without her.

"And you're going to be the star witness in the case against Esther Vamana and all the criminals who threatened you, terrorized you and took over your farm," Jay said. "It's done. It's over. We've won."

Which was probably true and yet didn't even feel the slightest bit like a victory. Something about his tone of voice and the frown on his face made her pretty sure he didn't feel that, either.

"But what about Franklin Vamana and the

Phantom Killer?" she said. "Has he been arrested? Have the bodies been found?"

"No," Jay said.

"And are you okay with that?" she asked.

"Of course I'm not," Jay said. "He taunted us, like a smug bullfrog, just knowing he'd gotten away with multiple murders he'd never get caught for. He dropped the kind of threats and comments that he knew any good lawyer would be able to get dismissed in a heartbeat as both hypothetical and insubstantial. Including vile threats against my colleague Jess, and her husband and children. He even implied my father begged for his life before he killed him—my father!"

He turned to Leia. An unexpected and anguished pain pooled deep in his eyes. "How could I ever be okay with knowing a man like that was out in this world living free? I thought that's what this case was about. I thought Franklin had sent the criminals to the farm to ransack it and kidnap you. Turns out I was wrong. It wasn't him, it was his sister. And that's okay."

No, it wasn't, in a way she didn't even know how to articulate. It wasn't all right that the Phantom Killer had gone unpunished.

"This wasn't how I thought this story was supposed to end," she said. "The Shadow gets caught. His prisoners get freed. There's no evil Shadow sister who turns out to be behind things all along."

"I know." Jay ran his hand over her back. Then he pushed the button again and the platform restarted its slow descent. "But not every story is going to end the way we want it to. And what can I do beyond keep digging at leads? Your sister Sally gave investigators a copy of your mom's stories and said she'll also use them to recreate her own maps of the locations in the story. Plus I have the ones I saved from your family's basement computer. Maybe this will give us new leads. I don't know. I just have to hold on to faith, pray and not give up. Sometimes the answers we get aren't the answers we hoped for, and together we brought multiple criminals to justice. We have to hold on to that."

She looked out over the twin Niagara waterfalls, one in New York and one in Ontario, as they crashed down into the basin below. She watched as the sun spread its gorgeous rays sparkling over the raging waters and casting shimmering rainbows in the spray. Raging waters swirled around tiny islands above the falls before then coursing between tall towering rock faces below, and she was reminded of all the people in history who braved that river to cross the border without detection, whether to escape slavery and war, embark on a new life or smuggle forbidden goods. Now, cars slowly moved back and forth along the Rainbow Bridge between the United States and Canada.

Shivers ran down Leia's limbs.

It couldn't be, could it? *Cymbafalls?* She grabbed Jay's hand.

"Stop the platform," she said, "and please tell me what you see."

Jay could hear his superior, the head of the operation, in his earpiece telling him that the building was secured and to hurry up and come down. They couldn't stay up there forever. Not to mention that, despite putting on a brave face, his wobbly legs were really looking forward to being back on solid ground. But something about the nervous joy filling Leia's voice had him pressing the button without hesitation. She squeezed his hand tightly.

"Okay, please don't think I'm crazy," she said, "but look at this view and tell me what you see."

She was excited about the view? Gamely he cast his eyes over the city below. He saw casinos and tacky tourist traps. There were billboards advertising a dinosaur-themed mini golf course, an upside-down house, an indoor water park and multiple ways to eat a lot of pancakes and steak for an incredibly low price. Traffic snarled and gawdy lights flashed.

"What am I supposed to be looking at?" Jay asked.

"You don't see it?" Leia asked. Her face fell.

"I see an eyesore," Jay admitted. Albeit one that had been built around a beautiful natural sight. "But I want to see what you see," he added. "Show me what I'm supposed to be looking at."

"It's a bit ridiculous," she said. Her shoulders rose and fell.

Her fingers began to slip from his, but he gripped them before they could fall.

"Please, Leia," he said. "What do you see?"

"I see Cymbafalls," she said.

"You're kidding," he said, and knew instantly that he shouldn't have. But he was beyond sore and exhausted from being awake almost twenty-four hours, and the words slipped through his lips before he caught himself. He'd actually thought she might be about to back down before he'd said that. But as soon as he spoke, he saw a fierce and beautiful defiance flash in her eyes.

She pulled her hand from his.

"Two waterfalls," she said, pointing, "side by side. A literal Rainbow Bridge joining them both, on top of the natural rainbows in the spray. There's a roaring river that pours into a chasm, islands and so many trees."

He opened his mouth but found that words failed him. Yes, all of those elements were technically there around them. But they were also swamped by fast-food restaurants, hotels and gambling.

"You're cherry-picking," he said, "and seeing what you want to see."

"Maybe," Leia said. "But your entire life is dedicated to seeing and finding the things nobody else can see. And if either your father or mine was here right now, wouldn't they both say that the Bible has countless stories, not to mention parables of Jesus, about treasures being hidden?"

He couldn't deny that, especially as Daniel 2:22 leaped immediately to mind. *He revealeth the deep and secret things: he knoweth what is in the darkness, and the light dwelleth with him.*

"Okay," he said, "when I told you that I was an undercover cop and that your dad had been helping me with a serial-killer cold case, you believed me. When I said he had a secret friend who'd seen the Phantom Killer murder someone and the evidence of that was hidden inside the house where you grew up, you didn't laugh at me, when maybe any sane person would have. So, let's say I believe you. Now what? We can't get a warrant without solid facts. And children's fairy tales won't cut it."

"So, we hop in a car and follow the clues," she said. "If we find something, you get a warrant to search it. If not, then all we've lost is a few minutes of driving."

She made it sound so simple. And if it had been anyone else he probably wouldn't have entertained the idea for a moment.

But just one look in Leia's eyes, and seeing the drive to fight shimmering there, was enough to make him feel like maybe he could, in fact, do the impossible.

"Let me talk to Jess… Detective Jessica Stone," he said. "She's the face of this operation and the one calling the shots. As you'll remember, she, her husband, Travis, and their tech-guru friend, Seth, were the ones I was trying to email for help. Sadly, our email didn't get through before the computer was blown to bits. But still, if anyone's going to have our backs on this, it's her."

"Okay," Leia said. Her chin rose. "But I'm really sure I'm not wrong."

Despite himself, he chuckled.

"What?" she asked.

"You remind me of Walter."

He started their descent again and finally the window-washing platform returned to the ground. Silently, Jay thanked God as he unclipped his harness and his feet stepped back on solid ground, and he prayed he would never have to go up anywhere that high outdoors for any reason ever again. He made sure Leia's harness was unclipped and that she was surrounded by good officers he trusted, and then he strode through the crowd, looking for his boss.

He found Jess in less than a minute, and after exchanging a status update on the case and arrests, he asked permission to commandeer an unmarked car and go for a drive with Leia.

"Why?" his supervisor asked.

He blew out a long breath.

"To go on a wild-goose chase to try to

find a secret Phantom Killer hideout because Niagara Falls reminds Leia of a location from her father's fairy tales," he admitted.

He expected his boss to laugh or point out the whole idea was ridiculous.

Instead, she crossed her arms.

"You really care about her, don't you?" she asked.

"Does that matter?" Jay asked.

She glanced to the sky for a moment and he had the distinct impression she was praying.

"Officially, I can't authorize a wild-goose chase," she said, "obviously. If you do find anything you think might be of interest to an active investigation or an ongoing crime, we need to proceed by the book if we want to make a case. But if you want to take a car and go for a quick drive I see no harm in that—just be back in thirty minutes."

"Okay," he said, and nodded. "Thank you."

"Now, unofficially," Jess said, "it doesn't take the world's greatest detective to see that you've got feelings for Leia. You've got this weird goofy grin that practically shouts it whenever you say her name."

Did he? Heat rose at the back of his neck.

He thought he'd hidden it pretty well from Leia's sisters, but they'd somehow noticed how he felt about her, too.

"Off the record," Jess went on, "I know a thing or two about being unable to admit how you feel about someone because of your work as a cop. Travis and I knew each other a long time before either of us were willing to admit how we felt. Then he burned out and quit the police force, while I stayed even more dedicated to my work. It took a long time to admit our feelings and figure out what our relationship would look like. All I'm saying is take the time and pray about what path you want your life to take. There are lots of ways to take down criminals and be a cop without giving up on love and a family. And if you care about this woman, maybe you should think that over."

His superior's words were still rattling like a loose screw ten minutes later as he and Leia were driving down the road that ran along the river. He cast a sideways look at her. Her cheeks were flushed with a happiness bordering on excitement. The light in her eyes left no doubt that this was going to work, and he didn't know how she could possibly have such confidence. After all, a few hours ago she'd been the skeptic and he'd been the one trying to convince her the Phantom Killer had been linked to her family. And now here she was singing little rhymes under her breath, reciting riddles and saying things like "Four giant oak trees, turn right here."

And here he was following her directions to the letter.

Lush vineyards lined the road to their left with the kind of houses he could imagine Franklin Vamana living in. Instead, she directed him to turn down a derelict service road to their right that ran between the train tracks and ugly buildings advertising cheap drinks and loud music. Then even those buildings disappeared, and they were back to following the river as it wound east away from the city.

"Stop here," she said. "This place on the right has to be it."

He looked up to see an abandoned gas station, with oil-stained pavement, shattered windows, dusty pumps and various abandoned car parts scattering the lot. This was the Shadow's fairy-tale castle? This was where Franklin Vamana, the Phantom Killer, had buried some of his bodies and left proof of his crimes?

He parked beside the building and got

out. She followed. The air smelled heavily of gasoline. He wondered what would happen if he called his boss and asked for a search warrant based on no evidence but nursery rhymes.

"Now," she said, "the ultimate treasure wasn't hidden in the castle—"

"Derelict gas station," he clarified.

"Because the Shadow was too tricky for that," she went on, like he hadn't spoken. "So he climbed down a steep cliff over the river and hid it in a cave." Her nose wrinkled. "Actually, it was more like a deep hole in the rocks. So, we have to find the path down the cliff and locate the hole."

When Jay didn't answer, she tossed her dark hair around her shoulders and started walking through the parking lot, past the building and all the way to the edge of the cliffside. He looked down at the raging rivers below. Sure enough, he could see what looked like a very narrow natural path that cut about ten feet down along the side of the cliff, where it disappeared into the rock.

"This whole treasure-hunt thing is a bridge too far, isn't it?" she asked. "I get it. After all, I grew up with my father's crazy survival drills and stories. It's okay if you don't believe it."

"Maybe I don't," Jay admitted. He turned to face her. "But I believe in you. At least, I believe that you're the smartest, bravest and most extraordinary person I know and that you'd never steer me wrong."

"And what if I am spectacularly wrong this time?" she asked.

"Then you can join the sometimes spectacularly wrong club," Jay said. "I'd rather be here and wrong with you than not take you seriously to begin with."

"Thank you," she said.

A smile filled her voice, and as she reached for his hand, everything in him wanted to pull her into his chest.

Instead, he gritted his teeth and stepped away.

"Judging by how narrow that path is only one of us can take it at a time," he said. "As the one with a badge, I'm calling it. After all, I'm the one who's going to make a case for getting a warrant. You stay up here. I'll leave you my phone, and if anything happens you call the police. Stay by the road where you'll be safer. Okay?"

"Got it," she said. "But what if you need the phone?"

"Don't worry," he said. "I got a second

one from my colleagues just to be sure. We're well-covered."

She nodded and her hands twitched like she wanted to throw her arms around him. But instead she stepped back. "Stay safe."

"You, too," he said.

He started walking down the narrow path, holding on to jutting rocks beside him for stability, while his mind debated whether or not there was even an actual path beneath his feet. The water below was a much shorter and safer drop than the farmhouse roof had been. The river ran much smoother than it had near the falls and he was a pretty strong swimmer. In fact, what worried him most about falling wasn't the possibility of drowning but the fact he'd be away from Leia for however long it took him to make it to shore somewhere he could pull himself up.

The path grew narrower until it completely disappeared not far ahead. He'd have to turn around somehow and head back soon. A wry grin crossed his mouth. Or he'd just have to walk up backward.

The police department's annual physical obstacle course, which he'd once been so worried about passing, was nothing compared to what he and Leia had faced in the last few hours. But somehow everything was different when Leia was around.

Loose rocks slipped underneath his feet. For a moment he lost his footing and had to grab on to a bush jutting out beside him to keep from falling. Okay, not a cave in sight and time to turn around. Jay shuffled his feet, trying his best to pivot on his toes. But stones kept sliding out from underneath him. He turned to face the cliff and tried to shimmy back up sideways.

Too late he saw the hole in the rock opening up beneath his feet, no wider than a plastic playground tunnel slide. His footsteps stumbled, then he slipped inside and tumbled into the darkness.

FIFTEEN

A long and sleek black town car pulled into the parking lot in front of Leia, blocking off the exit. Two large men in crisp black suits sat in the front seat. She'd never seen them before. But she knew they were the type to be incredibly professional and polite up until the moment their boss ordered them to hurt someone.

The back door opened, and Franklin Vamana leaned out.

"Get in," he said. "We need to talk."

It wasn't a question; it was an order. And somehow she knew that if she got in the car, this one conversation would be her last.

"No, thank you," she said, and stepped back. "I've already been abducted far too many times in the past few hours. If you have anything to say to me, you can come out here."

He smirked. It surprised her how angry

and hateful a smile could be. She glanced back over her shoulder toward the cliff where Jay had disappeared.

Jay, where are you?

Franklin got out of the car slowly, leaning on a walking stick. Immediately, he was flanked by the two scary-looking bodyguards in suits. Leia reached slowly into her pocket for the phone Jay had given her to call the police.

"Get your hands up!" Franklin snapped. "Whatever you're carrying, drop it."

He signaled the men in a swift, sharp moment. In an instant, one had turned a gun on her. The other stepped up and patted her down, taking the phone away.

Then Franklin just stood there and stared at her coldly for a long moment, with a look that she somehow knew had terrified and intimidated countless people before her. And to her surprise she crossed her arms and stared back at the man dressed in the suit that cost more than she'd ever make in a year. She thought about the billions of dollars he was worth and the people he'd ruthlessly killed. She considered the threats and taunts that Jay said he'd made when police had raided him a few hours earlier.

She thought of Jay.

And as she did, courage flowed over her. She realized, for the first time in a long time, that she wasn't afraid. Not of the killer in front of her who was probably her biological father. Not of the things he might be capable of, or the fact she might not make it out of his clutches alive. Because no matter what happened to her now, Jay would make sure he saw justice and was stopped.

"What are you doing here?" Franklin asked. He sounded genuinely puzzled. "How did you even know about this place?"

So, this was something here.

"My mother told me," she said. Her chin rose. "She left clues to this location in fantasy stories she wrote for my sisters and I before she died. The police have those stories now. It's only a matter of time before they find this place, too."

Not that she had any idea where exactly she was or why it was so important. But from the way Franklin's face went pale it was clear he did. She watched as his eyes darted from her, to the river, to the car and back, like he was doing some kind of re-calculation.

"So, you really are Ann-Margret Herber's daughter," he said finally. There was a faint hint of disgust in his voice, like he'd apprised Leia and found her lacking. Something menacing flickered in his gaze. "To be honest, I don't really remember her and didn't know she'd had you."

Somehow she knew he was lying. That he'd never forgiven her mother for defying him and was too proud to admit that for all the success he'd had in life one woman, her mother, had escaped his clutches. This was a man who expected to be feared and obeyed. He wanted people to fall before him in pain and fear. And somehow she knew that the best weapon she had against his attempts to scare her right now was the stubborn defiance the father who'd loved and taught her had instilled inside her heart.

Franklin Vamana might try to break her, but she would not fall. He was the Shadow and she'd spent her whole life knowing that evil men like him existed. She also knew that evil could be beaten and always would be in the end.

Franklin turned and walked toward the abandoned building. The bodyguard to his right was carrying a silver briefcase and the other was nudging her along with the muzzle of a weapon at her back.

"I have to admit I wasn't expecting to find this place," Franklin said, "let alone you.

But your mother remembered enough about this place, after she ran out on me that she was able to actually guide you here. Seems I pegged her all wrong. I thought she was too smart and obedient to tell anyone what she'd seen. What else did she tell you?"

She didn't answer. His scowl deepened. Franklin signaled to the man with the briefcase, and he brought it over. Franklin opened it slowly to show the high-powered explosive device lying within.

Her heart stopped. What could possibly be hidden here that was worth detonating a bomb to erase? Where was Jay?

Help me Lord!

"Cat got your tongue?" he sneered. "It doesn't matter. Everything you've found here is about to be destroyed. Every piece and scrap will disappear into dust and fall with the rockslide into the river. Because neither you nor your mother will ever bring me down."

Slowly Jay opened his eyes. The air around him was dark, clammy and as silent as a tomb. He looked up to see a grey circle of light far above him from the hole where he'd slipped through. How far had he fallen? How long had he been unconscious?

He didn't know. But his chest ached like his heart was being squeezed by an invisible fist at the thought that he'd left Leia alone up there. He forced his sore limbs to stand. He could feel his fake beard was half-hanging from his face and he tore it off the rest of the way.

"Hello! Leia!" He shouted up toward the light. "I need help! I've fallen into some kind of hole!"

His voice echoed around him. Silence came from the hole above and he realized he couldn't even hear the river anymore.

Lord, help me find my way out of this!

Thankfully his gun was still in its holster, but his phone was missing from his pocket. Desperately, he searched the floor and found his phone a moment later. But he could tell in a touch that the glass screen had shattered, and he couldn't get it to turn on. The pain tightened in his chest.

He felt for the wall, hoping to find a way to climb back up. But damp earth broke off in his hands.

"Hello!" he called as loudly as he could. "Leia!"

No answer came but his own voice echoing back at him from every direction. Whatever hole he'd fallen into sounded much bigger than he'd realized at first.

He pressed his hand against the wall and followed it in the darkness, planning to get a feel for just how large the hole was and anything like roots or rocks he could use as hand and foot holds to climb back out. Instead, as he walked the room seemed to expand beneath his touch until he found himself in what seemed to be a hallway. The walls turned from wet earth to rough brick. The tiny pinprick of light disappeared leaving the air pitch black around him. He reached up and felt a roof barely a foot above his head.

His heartbeat quickened. Each thud was so painful they seemed to momentarily steal the breath from his lungs.

Come on man! You're already afraid of heights. Since when do closed dark spaces rattle you, too?

But even as he chided himself, he knew exactly what it was that had made him able to climb up a roof or go up the side of a building in a window-washer basket.

Leia.

Her face floated before his mind's eye in the darkness. He remembered the strength and courage that had flashed in her beautiful violet eyes as she'd stood in the living room when he'd been captured and demanded the criminals leave her house and let him go. He thought about the deep and ferocious compassion that filled her face as she'd run from the flames with her sister's baby in her arms. And how she'd stood up for herself and challenged him when she thought he was out of line.

He felt braver, bolder and capable of being a better man when she was near than he could ever be without her. And now, with nothing but darkness around him, there was nothing left to distract him from letting the full impact of the myriad feelings he'd been pushing away hit him like a wave. Starting with shame at how he'd treated her. How had he let himself selfishly pull her into his chest so many times all while telling himself that he was going to let her go again? She deserved so much better than a man who was too afraid of how his own heart felt about her to admit it.

The truth was that he loved her. Over the past few hours since she'd first collided into his arms in the passageway, the small seeds of attraction and care that he'd been harboring in his heart for her had taken root and started to grow into the kind of feelings a man could risk his future on.

That he wanted to risk his future on.

Lord, I want to love Leia and let myself be loved by her. I'm so used to shutting my heart down I don't even know if I'm capable of it. And I don't have any idea what this means for my career and my future. But I don't want to be the man who pushes her away or hides the truth from her anymore. If I make it out of here alive, help me be the man who loves her the way she deserves.

The wall turned sharply at a left angle, and he stumbled into what felt like a cellar. Okay, now what was this? He ran his hands along the brick until he hit what felt like a tall metal shelf mounted to the wall. If he got it loose maybe he could use it as a ladder. He gave it a hard tug, then barely managed to leap back as it gave way and crashed to the floor ahead of him in a deafening clang, spilling its unseen contents across the floor.

He crouched down, felt around the mess and came up with some kind of rope, a pipe, a small shovel and finally a heavy-duty flashlight. He switched it on and blinked at the sudden bright light.

He was standing in a small room, about

five feet wide. Then he shone the light around the room and his heart stopped— there were piles of smooth white bones arranged neatly on shelves. A heavy and reinforced door lay to his right, but there was no doorhandle on his side and no way to budge it open. A large and dusty metal box, like a huge mechanic's toolbox, sat in the middle of the room. It was fastened shut with a lock, but it only took a few good stomps to break the latch off. He nudged it open with his foot. It was full of wallets, name tags and keys.

Fear ran like cold water through his veins. He'd told Leia that most serial killers kept souvenirs from their victims, feeling too arrogant to believe they'd ever be caught.

But nothing in his training had prepared him for this. He was standing inside the Phantom Killer's lair.

He crouched down, careful not to touch the evidence as much as possible. A sob rose in his throat. One of the licenses belonged to his father.

Leia had been absolutely right when she'd insisted they come here. They'd found the killer's lair, and he'd left her alone, outside and unprotected.

SIXTEEN

"You do understand that while some people won't understand everything I did, none of it was actually wrong, don't you Leia?" Franklin asked. His voice was an ugly mixture of arrogance and a pitiful need to be agreed with. "I would've done right by your mother and taken care of you if she'd told me the truth. It's not my fault she ran away."

Leia had no idea just how long she'd sat on a metal folding chair in the middle of a filthy and abandoned gas station, with her hands tied behind her back and some kind of suicide vest strapped to her front. But Franklin had spent the entire time talking, like he was some kind of monarch and she was a subject of his kingdom he thought he could berate and cajole in turn until she told him that he was right and begged him for mercy. He'd paced and yelled. He'd pulled up a chair opposite her and tried to sound like he'd be reasonable if she'd just submit to his authority. He'd gotten inches from her face and shouted.

And all the time, the bomb on her vest ticked down.

Franklin had made sure the henchman who'd wired her up had positioned the timer on her chest so that he could read how much time she had left and Leia couldn't. It was clear he enjoyed being the one in control.

How courageous her mom must've been to escape him.

"See, this gas station was my first real property purchase," Franklin said. "I was going to build a club. But I was only eighteen, and the real estate agent was a crook and didn't tell me the soil was contaminated from the gas and I wouldn't be able to get zoning. That's why I used this place to bury the things I didn't want anyone else to find. Then when my entertainment empire really began to take off in Toronto, there were all these people who just kept trying to ruin it for me. Worthless, filthy people who nobody cared about and contributed nothing to this world. Drunks, beggars, drug users, people who'd do anything for money—"

"People who had friends, coworkers and families!" Leia's voice rose. "People who were loved and made in the image of God."

The least of these.

The faces of his victims on Jay's crime board filled her mind. Her father and mother had instilled deep inside her that every person had value and to fight for those in need. She'd decided to dedicate her career to that. Jay had dedicated his life to that, too.

Hot tears filled her eyes.

Oh Jay, where are you now? Whatever happens to me, please be safe.

"You don't understand," Franklin started.

"I think I do!" she said. "My father taught me my entire life about evil people like you, who think they can just treat others as disposable and throw them out like the trash. Well, you're wrong. I'm proof of that. Because those people you killed were never forgotten and whatever you've got hiding here will be found. You're not some phantom or a shadow, let alone some king who gets to decide who deserves to live and who dies. And no matter what you do here today and what happens to me, you will be found and you will face justice."

A look turned in his eyes that was so dark for a moment she thought he was about to slap her. Instead he leaned forward and pressed a button on her suicide vest. The bomb beeped loudly.

"You don't deserve my pity or under-standing," he said. "You think some pa-thetic country farm girl like your mother and her unwanted daughter could bring me down? Well, you're too late. Because when the timer goes off it will all be gone. If you'd been willing to ask nicely and promise me you'd behave for me, I might have been will-ing to take you with me before it explodes. But now, I'm going to leave you here, tied up, to be destroyed with the rest of the gar-bage buried below you."

She pressed her lips together, raised her eyes to the skies and prayed. Psalm 31:5 filled her heart. *Into thine hand I commit my spirit: thou hast redeemed me, Oh Lord God of truth.*

"You have no idea who you're dealing with," Franklin snapped. "Or what I'm ca-pable of!"

"But I do!" Suddenly Jay's voice overtook the air. She turned and there he was. Jay was filthy and disheveled, his fake beard gone and dirt streaked his face. He looked like he'd been buried alive. But with a brighter light than she'd ever seen before shining in his eyes. Then he met her eyes, and a look that covered more than a thousand words could ever say moved between them. Jay aimed his gun at the killer he'd never given up on one day bringing to justice. "I know you're a cold-blooded killer who murdered almost a dozen people. I've seen your cave of sick trinkets and souvenirs. And I've called my colleagues from one of the phones I found. The police are on their way."

Franklin snapped his fingers as one of his bodyguard's stepped in between Franklin and Jay's gun.

"You can't win," Franklin said. "My bodyguards won't let you kill me. There's a bomb strapped to Leia and only I know the code to deactivate it. Your only option is to drop your weapon and let us go."

Jay did so and raised his hands. His fists clenched tight.

Franklin snickered. "Any last words?"

"Yes." Jay opened his palm, showing the golden badge in his grasp. "I'm Officer Jay Brock of the Ontario Provincial Police. Franklin Vamana, you are under arrest for the murder of my father, Jayce Starling…"

Something swelled in his chest as Jay stared down the Phantom Killer and named all of his victims, one by one—*Jonathan, Nathaniel, Calvin, Janet, Electra, Marissa*—reminding Franklin of the people he'd killed and the lives he'd stolen. Then he heard the thrumming of helicopters and saw the cars swarming down the road toward them as police rushed onto the scene before he could even finish reading Franklin the charges. Doors opened and police poured out, surrounding Franklin and his bodyguards.

Jay almost laughed. He'd gotten through to Jess a good fifteen minutes before he'd found his way out of that hole and they'd made it in time. *Thank You, God!*

He ran for Leia, pulled his pocketknife and cut her hands free. She leapt from her chair. Her panicked eyes met Jay's.

"How much longer is left on the timer?" she asked.

He glanced down at the bold red numbers on her chest. "Forty-two seconds."

For one agonizing second her gaze locked on his face. Her lips parted, but no words came out. Then she turned and ran, bolting through the arriving officers and making a beeline for the river.

And suddenly he knew what was going to happen, she was about to jump into the water to save them all.

"Leia! Wait!" Jay shouted. He ran after her.

"It's too late!" she called. "They'll never be able to defuse it in time!"

He gritted his teeth. She was the most stubborn and courageous person he knew. And he loved it about her. She reached the edge of the cliff.

"I love you, Jay!" she leapt.

But he caught her by the arm and yanked her back before she could fall.

"I love you, too," he said. "More than you'll ever know. Now, hold still and let me try to save you."

"But if the bomb goes off—"

"Then I'll die with you."

Desperately he hacked at the straps binding her with his pocketknife, slicing and cutting at anything he could reach. Finally, the shoulder straps tore. She wriggled free. He wrapped one arm around her waist and hurled the bomb vest toward the Niagara River.

"Maybe, you disarmed it—" she started.

An explosion filled the air. Water and dirt rose up around them like a plume. He pulled her into his chest and she wrapped her arms around him. Then, slowly they walked back from the edge.

"You know, out of everything my dad taught me," Leia said, "I never learned how to defuse a bomb."

He tossed his head back and laughed. Relief coursed over him like a wave.

"Where were you?" she asked.

"I fell into a hole and found the souvenirs of his victims," he said. "Bones, too. Exactly where you told me to look. I found a phone with a working battery and used it to call for backup. Then I used a metal shelf as a ladder. It wasn't quite high enough, but I managed to grab some roots and rocks from there and climb back out."

"I'm just glad you're alive," Leia said.

"You were right," Jay said. "About everything. I found the cave where he kept the souvenirs of all his victims. And you're right, it's more like a hole. But we'll get the forensic team down here to process the evidence and then we'll start using it to put together a case. It's finally over and it's all thanks to you." He took her face in his hands. "And I meant it when I said I love you. I know you don't have any reason to trust me, but I promise that whatever I felt for you last summer is nothing compared to what's grown between us in the past day."

He leaned forward to brush a kiss over her lips, but she stepped back. She started to walk back toward the police, and he followed.

"What about your career as an undercover detective," she asked.

"I don't know," he said. "But I know I love you."

Her head shook.

"You keep saying that," she said. "But are you sure you're not just swept up in emotions? We've gone through so much craziness in the past day. Love isn't just words, it's actions. I don't just need a man who'll throw himself into danger for me. I need a man who loves me enough to come home to me every night."

They kept walking in silence. She doubted he really loved her? Was she right?

"Leia!" Franklin's voice rose to a plaintive shout. "Leia! I demand to see my daughter."

She turned toward him, but Jay grabbed her arm. "Don't let him manipulate you."

"I won't," she said.

Jay followed her as she strode, head high, toward the handcuffed killer, through the crowd until she and Franklin were face-to-face again.

"You had a whole lot of words to say to me earlier," Leia told him. "Now I'm going to say my piece to you. Your sister says you are sick. If you do need a donor at some point in the future, write to me and let me know. I'll get tested, and if I'm a match, I'll pray about what to do next. Either way, I will pray for you every day for the rest of my life, and if you ever find salvation from your ways, feel free to let me know." She leaned toward him, and for the first time since Jay had laid eyes on him in Toronto, the sneer was gone, leaving nothing but a tired and broken man beneath. "But let me get this straight. I am not your daughter and you are not my father. I had a father, and his name was Walter. He gave everything he had to love me and guide me. And I will always be his child."

Then she turned away, leaving him spluttering and to be driven away by police before he could say another word.

She walked over toward the water, away from the gathered crowd, and silently Jay followed her. She stopped and her shoulders shook. Wordlessly he wrapped his arms around her, and she leaned back against him.

"I spent so much time being frustrated with my dad for being the way he was," she said. "It was like he was afraid of what would happen if he just let my sisters and I live our lives. I was hoping that maybe, when all this was over, I'd fully understand and agree with every decision he made. But I just can't."

"I know how you feel," Jay murmured softly into her hair. "When I discovered

Franklin's lair of souvenirs, I found my father's wallet and press credentials. I thought that maybe if I proved that the Phantom Killer really had murdered him…"

His voice trailed off.

"Then you'd know he'd been right all along and you wouldn't have to forgive him for the mistakes he'd made?" Leia asked softly.

"Yeah." He nodded. "I was hoping for some kind of perfect, complete answer where I wouldn't have to forgive him."

"Me, too."

"I don't know how I feel right now," he confessed. "It's like this big thing I've been chasing has come to an end, and I'm not sure who to even be now."

"I get it," Leia said, "and I don't have any answers. But I think we should take some time away from each other, until we're really sure we know how we feel."

He hugged her for a long moment while police moved around them, securing the scene. His heart felt heavy in his chest. *Lord, she's right. I can't just say I love her. I have to step up and be the man she needs me to be. I just don't know.*

Finally she pulled away and said goodbye. He stepped back and let her go.

SEVENTEEN

The sun was setting as Leia sat on the ledge of the attic window, with her feet on the slanted roof; she looked out the window below. It had been the longest day in her life and even though she'd slept a few hours in her own bed when she'd finally made it home from the crime scene in Niagara Falls, her body still ached with fatigue.

She thanked God she was safe and wasn't alone. Her sister Sally had met her at her Toronto apartment with Mabel and drove her back up to the farmhouse to collect her car. When she got there, she'd been surprised to find that not only had the police already finished with the crime scene, her sisters Quinn and Rose had flown from across the country to surprise her. They surveyed the damage left by the criminals and had already contacted insurance and started developing a plan to get the farm back on track.

All they needed now was to find and hire a farmhand.

Leia closed her eyes and let the final rays of the setting sun wash over her.

Lord, I have so much to thank You for that I don't know where to start. Heal our farm, heal our hearts and let Your justice continue to flow over our lives, this world and all we touch.

A confident meow came from behind her. She opened her eyes and turned around to see Moses leap through the open hatch and stalk toward her across the floor with a bright blue collar and tags around his neck. The cat leaped past her and disappeared down the roof. An instant later, Jay's head appeared through the hatch.

"I hope it's okay I got him a collar," he said. He climbed through the hatch and into the attic. "One of the other cops found him strolling around their ranks at the bottom of the Niagara Falls building, like he was part of the squad. I told them I'd take him back home."

She slid over to make room for Jay on the window ledge. But instead of swinging his legs outside onto the roof like she had, he sat with his back to the sky, his feet inside the attic and his face looking into hers.

"Why the collar?" she asked.

"So if he ever gets lost again he'll know his way home," Jay said. "You'll never guess who showed up at the regional police station and turned himself in this morning," he added. "Ben! He wanted to confess everything and help in the case in any way he could. He also said that you'd promised to help him find a lawyer."

"I did," she said. "He reminded me of so many other people who'd gone down the wrong path. I wanted to give him an opportunity to help turn his life around."

"Well, looks like he's taking it," Jay said. He looked down at their joined hands and then up into her face. "I also want you to know that I've decided not to continue being an undercover officer. It's the right job for a lot of people, but not for me. I think I was drawn to the idea of hiding from the past by pretending to be someone I wasn't. But I've decided that the past isn't as important as the future. And you are my future, Leia. It's so obvious and true, and I feel like I've known it forever. And those aren't just words. I've already started to put them into action. I've spoken to a grief counselor about getting help for processing the death of my father and the unhealthy ways I dealt with it in the past. He knows I also want to get help working through everything we've learned about your past, too. And I've spoken to my mentor about switching to a kind of investigative work that lets me come home to you every night. I really want to do this right."

Joy swelled in her chest.

"What are you saying?" she asked.

"I'm saying that I'm in love with you," he said. "I knew I loved you and wanted to marry you since the day we met, and all I've been doing since then is arguing with myself, because I never expected to find a woman as beautiful, incredible and extraordinary as you. I'm in awe of you, Leia."

"I'm in awe of you, too," she said. "I love everything about you."

"I'm a better man when you're with me," he said. "And I don't know what career path I'm going to take yet. All I know is that I won't stop fighting to take down criminals every day, with everything I've got, and that I'll be coming home to you every night. And one day, when you're ready, I'm going to ask you to marry me and start that new life together."

She reached up and cradled Jay's face in her hands, letting her fingertips run through his hair.

"I'm ready today." Her voice caught in her throat. "I want to marry you, Jay. I always have and I always will."

"I want to marry you, too," he said.

"Good," she laughed. "Because I don't want to live another day without you."

Then he kissed her, and she kissed him back, knowing for the first time with absolute certainty that their story would have a happy ending.

* * * * *

*If you enjoyed this story,
please look for these other books
by Maggie K. Black:*

Runaway Witness
Witness Protection Unraveled
Christmas Witness Conspiracy

Dear Reader,

Writing this story was so much fun, and I smiled through every page because it's full of memories of people I loved dearly. As I mentioned in the dedication, someone I loved passed away just a few weeks ago. I've only lost a few people in my life, including my grandparents, who I've been missing even more as the years go by.

This friend gave me the first spark of an idea for *Killer Assignment*'s hero, Mark; he was there when I saw the hockey stick tree that inspired *Christmas Blackout*, and he played at my first book launch. He was one of the most important storytellers in my life.

My first and most significant storyteller was my grandfather. When I was little, he told me bedtime stories about the farm where he grew up with his two sisters and five brothers. Pieces of him linger in so many of my heroes. Every truck mentioned in my books comes from memories of him, and he confidently climbed on the roof to fix the shingles in his seventies.

Thank you again to all of you who've sent me letters and messages! I don't check Facebook often but love to log in and see your messages.

You can reach me on Facebook and Twitter at @maggiekblack and email me through my website: www.maggiekblack.com. Thanks as always for sharing the journey with me.

Maggie

Get 4 FREE REWARDS!

We'll send you 2 FREE Books plus 2 FREE Mystery Gifts.

Love Inspired Suspense books showcase how courage and optimism unite in stories of faith and love in the face of danger.

FREE Value Over $20

YES! Please send me 2 FREE Love Inspired Suspense novels and my 2 FREE mystery gifts (gifts are worth about $10 retail). After receiving them, if I don't wish to receive any more books, I can return the shipping statement marked "cancel." If I don't cancel, I will receive 6 brand-new novels every month and be billed just $5.24 each for the regular-print edition or $5.99 each for the larger-print edition in the U.S., or $5.74 each for the regular-print edition or $6.24 each for the larger-print edition in Canada. That's a savings of at least 13% off the cover price. It's quite a bargain! Shipping and handling is just 50¢ per book in the U.S. and $1.25 per book in Canada.* I understand that accepting the 2 free books and gifts places me under no obligation to buy anything. I can always return a shipment and cancel at any time. The free books and gifts are mine to keep no matter what I decide.

Choose one: ☐ **Love Inspired Suspense Regular-Print** (153/353 IDN GNWN) ☐ **Love Inspired Suspense Larger-Print** (107/307 IDN GNWN)

Name (please print)

Address   Apt. #

City   State/Province   Zip/Postal Code

Email: Please check this box ☐ if you would like to receive newsletters and promotional emails from Harlequin Enterprises ULC and its affiliates. You can unsubscribe anytime.

Mail to the **Harlequin Reader Service:**
IN U.S.A.: P.O. Box 1341, Buffalo, NY 14240-8531
IN CANADA: P.O. Box 603, Fort Erie, Ontario L2A 5X3

Want to try 2 free books from another series! Call 1-800-873-8635 or visit www.ReaderService.com.

*Terms and prices subject to change without notice. Prices do not include sales taxes, which will be charged (if applicable) based on your state or country of residence. Canadian residents will be charged applicable taxes. Offer not valid in Quebec. This offer is limited to one order per household. Books received may not be as shown. Not valid for current subscribers to Love Inspired Suspense books. All orders subject to approval. Credit or debit balances in a customer's account(s) may be offset by any other outstanding balance owed by or to the customer. Please allow 4 to 6 weeks for delivery. Offer available while quantities last.

Your Privacy—Your information is being collected by Harlequin Enterprises ULC, operating as Harlequin Reader Service. For a complete summary of the information we collect, how we use this information and to whom it is disclosed, please visit our privacy notice located at corporate.harlequin.com/privacy-notice. From time to time we may also exchange your personal information with reputable third parties. If you wish to opt out of this sharing of your personal information, please visit readerservice.com/consumerschoice or call 1-800-873-8635. **Notice to California Residents**—Under California law, you have specific rights to control and access your data. For more information on these rights and how to exercise them, visit corporate.harlequin.com/california-privacy.

LIS21R2